Grimey Ways 3

**Lock Down Publications and Ca$h
Presents**

Grimey Ways 3
A Novel by *Ray Vinci*

Lock Down Publications
P.O. Box 944
Stockbridge, Ga 30281

Visit our website @
www.lockdownpublications.com

Copyright 2023 by Ray Vinci
Grimey Ways 3

First Edition February 2023
Printed in the United States of America

This is a work of fiction. Names, characters, places, and incidents either are products of the author's imagination or are used fictitiously. Any similarity to actual events or locales or persons, living or dead, is entirely coincidental.

Lock Down Publications
Like our page on Facebook: Lock Down Publications @
www.facebook.com/lockdownpublications.ldp

Book interior design by: **Shawn Walker**
Edited by: **Jill Alicea**

Stay Connected with Us!

Text **LOCKDOWN** to 22828 to stay up-to-date with new releases, sneak peaks, contests and more…
Thank you.

Submission Guideline

Submit the first three chapters of your completed manuscript to ldpsubmissions@gmail.com, subject line: Your book's title. The manuscript must be in a .doc file and sent as an attachment. Document should be in Times New Roman, double spaced and in size 12 font. Also, provide your synopsis and full contact information. If sending multiple submissions, they must each be in a separate email.

Have a story but no way to send it electronically? You can still submit to LDP/Ca$h Presents. Send in the first three chapters, written or typed, of your completed manuscript to:

LDP: Submissions Dept
Po Box 944
Stockbridge, Ga 30281

DO NOT send original manuscript. Must be a duplicate.

Provide your synopsis and a cover letter containing your full contact information.

Thanks for considering LDP and Ca$h Presents.

Ray Vinci

Chapter 1

Quick had just finished counting up all the money he had to his name. Altogether, he had a little bit over $200,000, and he planned on spending it on some work. He had to get his weight up if he planned on taking over San Antonio. Even though Kilo and his homies were locked up, he still had to deal with Babygurl and her squad. Babygurl was a female version of Kilo, if not worse, plus the team of hoes she had would ride with her until their deaths. And that's exactly what Quick had planned to give them, but it took money and a loyal team. He had been plotting for the last three weeks since Correy had been locked up but came up with nothing.

He had yet to get in contact with Pablo because right about now, he didn't know who to trust. As he stacked up his money, he felt his phone vibrate in his pocket. He pulled it out and saw that it was Lexi. He ignored it, then went back to stacking the money. He had been ducking Lexi and Lovey for the past week and a half because he couldn't think around them nagging-ass hoes. All Lovey did was complain about Correy, and Lexi was just annoying as fuck with all that scary-ass shit. He had a spot on Detrich Road that nobody knew about, so he had been kicking it there for a little bit so he could get his mind right.

He lit a Newport and took a deep pull, then let the smoke settle in his lungs. He jumped in the dopefiend rental and decide to roll around San Antonio to see what he could come across. His first mission was to find a team of shooters that was trained to go at any given moment. Second, he would see what spots he could set up at.

He pulled up to the Chevron on I-35 and New Braunfels to fill up his gas tank and to buy some Newports and cigars. As soon as he jumped out, a beat-up Toyota pulled up next to him. Once he saw who jumped out, a smile ran across his face so fast he didn't realize he was doing it.

"Savage, is that you?" Quick said as the nigga turned his way.

"My motherfuckin' nigga Quick, what's good?" said Savage.

Savage represented his name to the fullest, but by far was one of the smartest street niggas that Quick had ever met. He was 6'2" and weighed 215 pounds and had a body full of tattoos. He had caramel skin, deep waves, and a swag out of this world. As Quick looked at him, he really couldn't believe what he was seeing. Savage always stayed in the latest fashion and cars. Savage was really a gangsta in a pretty boy's body, but from the looks of it, he needed to be put back up to the status he held a couple of years back.

"Damn, gangsta, what type of shit you got going on? I ain't never seen you looking like this," Quick said while his mind was already doing numbers.

"Shit, I got hit about a year ago by some niggas and they hit me for everything. Shit, the niggas that was on the team dipped and the li'l connect I had took off because I fucked his money and work off," Savage said while he went to show Quick some love.

"So, what you trying to do now? Because I'm tryna build me a stomp down team to take this bitch over."

"If it got anything to do with any kind of money, you know I'm down."

"Most definitely. But at the end, it's gon' be an all-out war because this shit is bigger than what it looks like," Quick said while looking him in the eyes to see if he still held his reputation of being a savage-ass nigga.

"Nigga, you must've forgot who the fuck you talking to. We was raised together, so you know what type of shit I do," he said with seriousness in his voice.

Once he said that, Quick smiled and nodded his head because he knew shit was about to start falling in place. "Look, hit my phone in like two days and we gon' take a little trip to the Westside. While I make these phone calls, I need you to grab some niggas and scope out some spots so we can set up shop."

"Shit, that's a bet, my nigga."

They exchanged numbers, then went in the store to grab what they needed. Then they went their separate ways.

***

Babygurl, Kiesha, Cassy, Ladie, and Sadie sat inside of Kilo's old trap on Skinnie's block with 160 bricks of cocaine in the back room. Before Kilo had got locked, he and the squad had copped eighty bricks and had hit Correy for everything he had. Money and spots wasn't the issue for them; it was finding a new connect, plus that nigga Quick was still going to be a problem. Kilo knew what Babygurl was doing when she started recruiting all of those bad bitches, and she planned on doing exactly was she intended to do from the jump, which was keep the squad's name ringing and take over every inch of San Antonio and everything around it.

Babygurl lit up a Sweet as she eyed all four of her homegirls. Out of all of them, she and Kiesha were the tightest, but she had love for all of them because when Correy and Quick had kidnapped her and beaten her half to death, they held her down. If it wasn't for Ladie and Sadie, she probably would have died, but they rode out to the end. She watched Kilo run the squad with ease, so she knew what she had to do. She hit the blunt one more time, then passed it to Kiesha as Cassy lit up another one.

"Alright, y'all, we got a room full of bricks of that drop and a city to hold down. At the same time, I want that bitch ass nigga Quick, plus we gon' need a connect. We got enough to last us for a couple of months, but if we want to hold the streets, we have to keep them flooded," Babygurl explained to her squad. They might have been five bad-ass bitches, but all of them were stone cold killas. "So, I need all of us to be on the lookout for a plug."

"Have you heard anything about the squad?" Kiesha asked.

"Yeah, Bianca said that the million dollars Kilo gave her is only gonna get him out. The only thing is, he has to leave the state. I got her setting up a li'l spot for him outside of San Antonio until we can find him somewhere to go. As far as the rest of the team, whatever money they got, we gon' have to put up the rest because we need them niggas out here with us."

As soon as she said that the front door opened and Bianca came in with a tight green Michael Kors dress that stopped at her thighs and some white Michael Kors heels. She was draped down in jewelry and her hair hung down to her fat ass, which they all swore was fake. It seemed like her green eyes were bright as hell due to her green dress. They were all bad, but she stood out because she was white. Bianca was Kilo's soon to be baby mama and lawyer, but she had promised to represent all of them, and in the matter of months she had saw millions of dollars and knew she was about to see a lot more with the way Babygurl was going.

"How you gon' tell all of us to meet up and that you had something you wanted to run by us, and you're late?" Cassy said.

"Yeah, I was tied up in court, but check this out. Before I let y'all know what I got planned, I've run this by Kilo and he approves, but he told me to run it by y'all to see what y'all think." She stopped, then looked at everybody. She knew she was good because of Kilo, but at the same time, Babygurl made her nervous because of Kilo. "With the way I know y'all about to turn up on Quick and these streets, shit is about to get real, real quick. So, I got two people who I know y'all gon' need to have on the team. They both are my cousins. One's another lawyer, and one's FBI. Kilo had y'all on point, but I promise with us on y'all's team, we can help y'all take the game to another level."

"And when do you plan on bringing them in?" asked Babygurl as she reached for one of the blunts.

"Right now." She texted something on her phone and a couple of minutes later, a female that looked exactly like her only with blue eyes, and a white dude that looked like he should have played power forward for the San Antonio Spurs, walked in.

"This is Valerie. She's a lawyer and is experienced in other things we can talk about at another time. This is Special Agent Robert Long. He heads a team of FBI agents that investigates Texas drugs lords, so he has the ins and outs as to what's going on in the streets as well as the investigation room."

Once she finished, she saw that Babygurl had a big-ass smile on her face, but before she could say something, Sadie spoke first.

"How the fuck we know y'all ain't tryna set us up?" said Sadie while standing up, and Ladie did the same thing.

"Damn, y'all sexy as hell!" Agent Long said.

They all started laughing because he sounded like he'd been around black people all his life. Casey was so quiet Babygurl almost forgot she was there. She lit up another Sweet, hit it a few times then passed it to Valerie who started coughing so hard that tears came out of her eyes.

"Look, y'all can disrespect me all y'all want, but Kilo knows what the fuck he is doing, and if y'all think I'm gon' sit up here while thinking he'll let someone try to take y'all down, y'all got me fucked up!" Bianca said while turning red. She was nervous as hell because she knew how all five of them got down, but Kilo was her man, and she refused to let anybody disrespect his name in front of her.

All Babygurl could do was smile and nod her head in approval. "Oh, we gon' get along just fine. I like what yo' country ass got going on, but how much is all of this gon' run us?"

"Me and Valerie can split our cut, which we'll talk about later. But he's gon' need fifty a month starting at the beginning of every month, so you got a few weeks in advance to get right."

"And just 'cause I'm sitting in a room full of bad bitches, I'ma hit y'all with a little tip. Quick is about to be plugged in with the Mexican Mafia, so y'all better be ready for what's coming," he said, then he set his card on the table and walked out.

All of them were surprised at what he said because they didn't know Quick was moving like that. Babygurl immediately started putting together a plan that she knew would work but would take some time. She and Valerie exchanged numbers and they all ended their night with a lot to think about.

Ray Vinci

Chapter 2

They had all promised to meet up at Bar 23 because it had been a while since they had any fun. Since Babygurl had been kidnapped, she had been laying low. She really didn't feel like going out, but Kiesha had convinced her otherwise. She needed to show her face to let motherfuckas know that she and her girls were running shit.

As she pulled up to the parking lot, she noticed that her girls had the back of the lot locked down. All of them were dressed down from head to toe so every nigga that was out was staring. Babygurl pulled next to Sadie's gold Lexus, then jumped out. She had on some black skintight Fendi pants with the black Fendi bloused to match and some black Fendi flats, just in case somebody wanted to trip. Her long curly hair hung down her back and stopped at her ass. The gold jewelry that draped her hands, neck, and ears caused much attention with the stares that her girls were already getting.

"Where's Ladie at?" she said as she looked around.

"She's behind the bar. Somebody had to get the straps in," said Sadie. Sadie and Ladie were bartenders at multiple clubs, which made it easy to get their burners in.

They walked straight to the door and Cassy handed the bouncer $500 to skip the line. Bitches was hating but didn't say nothing because most of them knew who Babygurl and her squad was. The bouncer let them in and the Megan Thee Stallion that was banging through the speakers instantly turnt them up. Babygurl looked towards the bar and spotted Ladie. Ladie nodded her head then pointed to the V.I.P. booth that sat in the corner. They all danced to the music as they made their way to the V.I.P. booth. Bottles were already sitting on ice thanks to Ladie. Babygurl looked behind the couch that was barely off the wall and saw the bag that she was looking for. Once she saw that, she relaxed as Kiesha poured Apple Ciroc in everybody's cups.

They back doored another Megan Thee Stallion and Sadie got up and started twerking. Sadie's ass was fat, so it was all over the place as niggas stood staring in their direction. Babygurl decided to put on a show with she and started shaking her ass right alongside of her. She spotted a nigga in the crowd that was dripping in jewelry and an iced-out grill, plus the Gucci he had on made him look like dollar signs. He waved Babygurl over, which made her and Sadie look at each other. She hesitated, then said fuck it as she and Sadie made their way to where he was. She looked back at Kiesha and Cassy, and they knew that look meant for them to watch their backs. When they made it to them, he and his team were standing around swagged in designer gear as well.

"What's up, li'l daddy? You waving a bitch over here and not sayin' nothing," said Babygurl.

"I'm just admiring the baddest bitches in the club. My name is Sean."

"I'm Babygurl. I see you looking like a million bucks, plus your team looking good. How about y'all come kick with us in the V.I.P?" she said, then she and Sadie walked off, making their asses shake because they knew they had their attention. Babygurl saw dollar signs and wanted to see what he had going on, plus the nigga was fine as hell with his long dreads and thick beard.

As soon as she sat down, he and his three homeboys began walking toward their booth. Her squad already knew what she saw in them because they saw it as well. Sean walked up and sat next to her as his homeboys found a seat next to her homegirls.

"How come I never see you around here? Where you from?" she asked as she handed him a bottle.

"We from Atlanta, shawty. My family moved on some change type shit, so me and my brother came with them."

"Oh yeah? And what y'all doing out here? Because I know y'all don't got no connections like that."

"You asked that like you can employ a nigga or something," he said as he scooted a little bit closer so they wouldn't be heard.

"I can turn you and your boys up more than you ever been, but I don't think you ready for what me and my girls got going on," she said as she inhaled his cologne. The nigga was sexy as hell and the way his deep voice was in her ear made her pussy wet.

"Oh yeah? I see you about your paper. I like what I'm hearing, shawty, but I don't think you got what I'm looking for."

"I can front you whateva you buy and put you in a spot," she said while looking him in his eyes to let him know she was serious. "Cool." He reached for her phone and plugged in his number. "But I'm tryna see what's up with you though. Can a nigga get a dance or what?"

She laughed, then pulled him up and walked to the dance floor. She instantly got to popping her ass on him to see if he could stand under that pressure. She grinded on his dick and was loving what she was feeling. Before she could turn around, she felt someone bump her shoulder.

"Bitch, you betta watch who the fuck you bumping into!" a short, thick yellow bone said with two of her homegirls next to her.

"Look, sis, you don't even want these problems, so you need to keep it moving," Babygurl said as she turn back toward Sean.

"Bitch, you got the game fucked all the way up. Yo' Mexican ass already in here dancing on our nigga, so it's best you keep it moving before we stomp yo' ass out this hoe," the girl said as all three of them inched close.

Kiesha, Cassy, and Sadie were already on point and made their way towards her.

"Last time I checked, this was my nigga, and the last time a bitch was talking stupid, I did the stomping——"

Before she could finish, she was rushed by ol' girl, but her being from the streets, she saw it coming and side-stepped her and slung her to the ground by her shirt. Kiesha, Cassy, and Sadie, plus Sean, his brother, and his two cousins were by her side in a heartbeat. The girl got up and posted up as Babygurl did the same. Babygurl wasted no time and hit her with what looked like a ten-punch combo as ol' girl fell. Babygurl landed right on top of her, then grabbed her hair as she slammed her head to the floor. Her girls started in on the other two as a crowd formed around them.

"I. TOLD. YO'. STUPID. ASS. TO. KEEP. IT. MOVING!" she said as she punched her face in.

The crowd began to split as two niggas came up and snatched Babygurl up. Sean knew that they weren't bouncers and stepped up.

"Naw, playboy, it ain't going down like that," he said.

"Nigga, it goes like however I want it to go," he said through clenched teeth.

As Sean stepped up, his cousins both stepped up and put straps to both their heads. They had paid off the bouncers to let them bring their bangers in the club.

"We don't even want no smoke, but if y'all want it, my family will light that ass up quick," said Sean. "Babygurl, y'all go get y'all shit and let's bounce."

Five minutes later, they were all in the parking lot, including Ladie, all turned up. Babygurl was chilling next to Sean when a group of niggas a few cars down started grilling them.

"Look like them niggas ain't feelin' what went down in the club," he said as he reached for his heat.

Once Babygurl saw him do that, she wasted no time reaching in her clutch purse and pulling out her all-black nine-millimeter. Their squad was on point and had their hands on theirs. Babygurl had to see if he and his boy was stomp down, so she was the first one to let loose on the group of niggas. Her squad started letting their guns bust and Sean and his niggas followed suit. Bullets lit up holes in the side of the cars as the niggas and bitches that was staring their way ducked behind them. The air was instantly filled with gunsmoke as they littered the parking lot with bodies and gun shells. They never eased up on their triggers until they ran out of bullets. Once they ran out, they all knew what time it was. Sean jumped in the car with Babygurl as his brother and cousin all jumped in his whip, and her squad did the same. Bullet holes were out in the side of Babygurl's all-white BMW as they all smashed out of the parking lot. She drove off while looking at Sean and knew she had a gangsta on her team.

***

Quick made the call he was supposed make and had set up a date and time to meet up, which was today. He was on his way to Muncey Street to pick up Savage so he could go with him, because he didn't know Pablo, plus he wanted to scope out the first area he would be taking over. Quick had thought he would be going back to the run-down house that he first saw Pablo at. Pablo had helped him hide from the police for a couple of days and when it was time to leave, Pablo told him to hit him up in a few days.

He pulled up to the all-white duplex and hit the horn twice. Savage came out looking like money because he knew what time it was. He jumped in Quick's blue CTS on 26" Forgiatos and was hit by the kush smoke. He dapped up Quick, grabbed the blunt, then leaned back as he hit it.

"Where to?" asked Savage.

"Shit, the Dominions!" he said as they drove off.

It took them twenty minutes to get to the Dominions and they were loving what they were seeing.

"Oh yeah, I've gots to come get me one of these big-ass houses," said Savage.

"No bullshit. Look, when we get in here, let me talk. Just have my back." He pulled up to the gate and hit the intercom button.

Pablo was already waiting on them, so he buzzed them in. Quick drove up the driveway straight to the door. They jumped out and were quickly relieved of their guns. Neither one said anything because they had been through this process before, plus Quick knew that Pablo was an important man. Once they entered the mansion, they both were in awe. They didn't get a chance to admire it and were quickly walked to a dinner table, where Pablo and two beautiful Mexican women sat as food was being brought in. Two chairs were empty and Quick and Savage sat in them, which was between what looked to be mother and daughter.

"Quick, it's good to see you. You looking way better than the last time I saw you," Pablo said as he lit a cigar.

"It's good to see you too, and the last time you saw me, I was in an unusual predicament. This here is my man, Savage," Quick said.

"Nice to meet you, Savage. This is my wife Maria and my daughter Jessica."

Quick and Savage nodded their heads while maids piled food on their plates.

"I'm glad we finally got the chance to meet up and do business. Now tell me about what caused you to jump over my fence that night."

While eating, Quick told him everything that he had going on with Correy and Kilo from day one. He didn't have to tell him everything, but he did, because he needed Pablo to trust him.

"So now you need a new connect because that fucker Escobar is a fucking snitch."

"Yeah. I got $200,000 in the car right now. I'm tryna take over this whole state, but first I need San Antonio, and I have to get this crazy-ass girl Babygurl out of the way," he said while finishing off the scotch that one of the maids had poured him.

Savage was sitting quietly and listening. He was loving the way his homie was conducting business. The whole time Quick was talking, Quick and Jessica would sneak glances at each other.

"How much can you handle?"

"Howeva much you can give me. You just heard me say I'm tryna take over Texas."

Pablo chuckled and nodded his head because he was starting to like Quick more and more. "Mijo, be careful what you ask for, because you might bite off more than you can chew."

"Me and my boy hungry, so there's no such thing as biting off more than I can chew," Quick shot back.

"Okay, mijo, in three days, a U-Haul will be coming your way with everything you need to start your little empire. Keep your money. All I ask for is loyalty, honesty, and respect. If you get into any kind of jam, just call me and my people will handle it." He snapped his fingers and a maid came and handed him a brown box that contained two Cuban cigars. She poured them some more scotch as Pablo, Quick, and Savage puffed and sipped to a new business deal.

"Congratulations. Welcome to the Mexican mafia," Pablo said with a smile.

Chapter 3

They had been waiting in a long-ass line for damn near two hours and were glad to finally be going in to see Correy. Lexi had only gone with Lovey because she was thinking about going to see Kilo, but then thought against it. This would be the first time they had come to see him since he has been locked up. It was going on a month since Correy and Kilo had been locked up, and she barely heard from Quick. Today was the first time she had heard from him in two weeks. He had given her $500 to put on his books, paid all her bills, and took them grocery shopping. He had told her to tell Correy to call him so they could set up a visit. They had him for aggravated assault with a deadly weapon on a peace officer. Quick had told her to get a good lawyer so they could try to get him out on bail.

They were led down a hallway to where the visit booths were, and they instantly remembered the days when they used to come see Correy and Kilo. Lovey never knew what had happened to make them fall off, but she figured it was serious because their baby sister Lisa had been killed because of it. She would never forgive Correy for that bitch Babygurl killing her sister because of the shit they had going on.

When they got to the booth, Correy was on the other side of the glass with some brand-new oranges and a fresh taper with his waves spinning 360°. Once he saw them, he smiled and then grabbed the phone, and Lovey did the same.

"Hey beautiful, you looking good," he said then nodded towards Lexi, who was holding her daughter Heaven. "How you holding up out there?"

"I'm good. Quick just paid all the bills and filled up the box with all kinds of food. He also gave me $500 to put on your books. But baby, I miss you," she said in a baby voice.

"I know, baby, but it's not looking too good for the home team."

"Quick told me to hit up a lawyer so we can at least try to get you out on bail."

"Speaking of a lawyer, I had one come through and told me she would fuck with me. Before we through, I'ma give you the info so you can give it to Quick," he said with a smile on his face. It was the best news he had heard since he'd been locked up. Detectives would come and try to get him to snitch on Kilo and his boys, but no matter how much he hated that nigga, he was far from a rat-ass nigga. And for what it was worth, he knew Kilo and his squad was stomp down, so he was good on that end.

It seemed like the little twenty-minute visit went by in five when you had a lot to talk about. By the time the visit was up, he gave her the number to the lawyer. He told her to tell Quick he would call and that he loved her.

A minute later, he was walking down the corridor when Officer Jones pulled him to the side out of earshot of the other officers. Officer Jones and Correy knew each other because he used to patrol the Landings and he let Correy do his thing while Correy paid him and put him on all types of pussy.

"Remember that nigga you told me watch out for?" asked Officer Jones.

"Yeah, what's good on that li'l situation ,Joe?"

"Well, that nigga sleeping in BL, and for the right amount, I can put the thumb on him for you."

"Cool. Hit my nigga and tell him to hit you with $5,000 for me, and make sure that gets done," he said, happy as a broke nigga in a room full of money. Today was a good day because he had been looking for that pussy-ass nigga since he'd been locked up. He had to be careful because this was Kilo's territory, so he knew Kilo was probably on the same shit. He walked down the hall with a smile on his face because shit looked like it was finally starting to go his way.

***

When Babygurl had peeled off from the club yesterday, night she went straight to her old apartment instead of the house she was living in with Kilo. The reason she did that was because she didn't want Sean to know where she really laid her head. She had been dead to the world all day and when she checked her phone to see what time it was, it read 7:25 p.m. She saw that her girls had been blowing up her phone and got up. She heard movement in her living room and instantly grabbed her 9mm. She made her way to the living room and when she saw Sean just getting up, she relaxed. When she saw him staring, she realized what she was wearing. She had on some pink booty shorts that showed her pussy print and that cut up in her fat ass to where her cheeks were hanging out, plus her white muscle T-shirt revealed she didn't have on a bra, so her titties hung out of the side. She also realized that she had her gun at her side, so she sat it down.

"My bad. I forgot you was here." She sat down on the other couch.

"It's cool. I probably would have done the same thing if I was you, shawty. Look, my li'l bro and cousins have been hitting me up all day. You think you can drop me of on the Northeast side so I can meet up with my fam?" He stared at her pussy print. He couldn't deny she was one of the baddest Mexican bitches that he had ever seen. All night he had contemplated robbing her, but with the way she and her squad of bad bitches handled their business last night, he thought twice, plus he wanted to see what type of shit she had going on.

"I'm not gon' lie, them niggas gon' have to wait because I got this li'l spot I'm tryna show you. Get dressed before a bitch be tempted to give yo' fine ass some pussy," she said, then went to take a shower.

He laughed as he watched her fat ass jiggle on the way to the back. He was tempted to go jump in the shower to see if she was really about what she was talking about. He got dressed in the same Gucci clothes he had on the other night, but it still looked like they came fresh off the racks. By the time he got himself together, Babygurl was still in the shower, so he decided to look around her spot a little bit. He liked the way she had her shit set up, but he could tell she hardly stayed there. Once he finished, he went back to the living room to text his family to let them know that he was good to meet him at the trap in a few hours.

When she stepped from the back, she was looking good as hell in her brown and khaki one piece Louis Vuitton suit that showed off every curve that she had. Her Alexander McQueen heels made her look taller than what she was, but she was still short and dangerous. Her hair was pulled back in a ponytail, so he saw how pretty she really was. Out of instinct, he pulled her into his arms and kissed her while he grabbed her ass cheeks. He inhaled her Fendi perfume and held her close.

"Let's get up out of here before I be tempted to put this dick on you."

"Please! 'Cause you got a bitch trippin' right now." She laughed as she walked out of the door.

They jumped in her BMW. She turned up the City Girls that was already in the deck, then peeled off to Kingspoint apartments. It was his first time riding through the Eastside and he realized it wasn't any different from East Atlanta. They pulled up to Jalisco's off of W.W. White Road, grabbed some tacos, then jumped back on the road.

"So what you got in mind when you say you can turn me and my boys up?" he said while eating his tacos.

"I can front you five birds. I need $20,000 off of everyone though," she shot back. "This li'l spot we about to stop at is one of the first spots that I came up in, and it gets no less than $10,000 a day. It's yours, if you think you can handle it."

He nodded his head because he was liking what he was hearing. He was doing the math in his head and for the five bricks she was coming off, of all he had to do was give her $100,000. She had to be getting to some money if she was showing him some love like that. He was glad that he had been eyeing her from the moment she had stepped inside of Bar 23. He most definitely had to find out more about her, and he had to test that pussy out.

They pulled inside of Kingspoint and parked at the front. She wanted him to get a feel of what he was getting into, because niggas would try him even if she was the one who put him on.

"I hope you ready for what you about to get into, because this shit is bigger than Nino Brown."

"Shawty, I've been doing this for a long time, and my guns bust just like yours if any one of these niggas feel like testing a nigga, ya feel me, mama?" He said with a serious look into his eye.

"I'm just saying, shit's about to get real."

Sean knew she was warning him of something, but he didn't even care because he was trying to get to some money. As they walked, he saw so many niggas and hoes that it reminded him of his projects back home where he grew up at. Everyone seemed to be showing Babygurl some love as she made her way to an apartment that had a couple of niggas sitting out front.

"What's up? Y'all got some of that fire up in there or what?" Babygurl asked.

One of them nodded his head and one went in to go get what she had asked for. While they waited, the nigga looked Sean up and down, then chuckled.

"So, what they talking about with the big homie Kilo?" he said to Babygurl.

"Everything all good on his end. We just tryna make sure he good wheneva his time comes, ya feel me?"

"Yeah. If he needs anything, let me know, and it's gon' get done. What's up with the homie right here?"

"I'm Sean, and I'ma be setting up shop in the back. And who might you be, li'l homie?" he said, speaking up for himself.

"I'm Li'l Mike, and this the kush spot, so if you need anything of that nature, holla at me," he shot back. "Damn, Babygurl, when you gon' put me on?"

"Kilo already put you on. I mean, you got everything on smash with the kush."

The li'l nigga that left for the doe-doe came back with her sack and some cigars. She didn't have to pay because Kilo made sure of that. She rolled one up, then lit it as they walked off. He looked back at Li'l Mike and knew that he was gon' be a problem, but he for sure didn't have a problem with filling his li'l smart ass up with some hot shit. Niggas was already trying to test his gangsta and he hadn't even started getting money yet. He already knew Li'l Mike was fucked up about her being with him, and that's why he brought up Kilo's name. She had passed him the blunt of kush and he inhaled it hard as he took in his surroundings.

"So, who is Kilo?"

"That's my ride or die since day one. He's the reason I'm set in the position I'm in to put you in the position you about to be in. But you don't have to worry about him ,because even though he'll always be my number one, we do our own thing."

He started laughing because by her tone, you could tell that talking about Kilo was a sensitive subject, so he left it alone.

They were halfway finished with the Sweet when they walked into the spot. Kiesha was sitting in the living room counting money and then stuffing it in the duffle bags that were sitting on the floor.

"Hell naw! I been blowing yo' phone up all day and night and the whole time you been getting some dick from this fine-ass chocolate nigga. Alright, don't make Kilo put some hot shit in that ass," she said as she snatched the Sweet from her hand.

"Girl, shut yo' stupid ass up. It ain't even like that, and Kilo don't run shit this way, plus I just gave him this spot so we can do some other shit."

Even though she said that about Kilo, she knew he would act a fool once Li'l Mike shot word back to him. She had to make sure shit was run her way, and she damn sure needed a bigger team.

She, Kiesha and Sean chopped it up some more about money, then they left so he could meet up with his family. She hoped she was making a good decision about putting him on. Little did she know Quick and a new connect were the least of her worries.

Chapter 4

Kilo sat in front of the TV with a hot cup of coffee while watching the San Antonio Spurs beat down the Houston Rockets. Even though he had been locked up for a little over a month, he was still making moves that benefited Babygurl and her squad. He had just gotten off the phone with Bianca, and she told him that she and Valerie were looking into the cases of Slugga, Illy, and Felony. He had even convinced her to send Valerie to represent Correy's bitch ass. He refused to let that nigga get away with what he had done to Babygurl. He knew it wouldn't be hard for all of them to get out because Detective Stronbone had fabricated the assault on a peace officer case. He would be out in a little less than a year, but he had to leave San Antonio, so he at least had to get his homies out. He also had another role for Valerie to play, but he had to talk to her on her own for that play. He knew she would be down because she was attracted to the life of a street nigga.

He noticed the day room had gotten quiet and looked back to see what the silence was all about. When he saw a group of niggas huddled up by the rec yard door staring his way, he knew he was the reason for the silence. There were four of them niggas in all, so he knew he was in a lose-lose situation. He didn't know what them niggas' beef was about, but he didn't give a damn. He drained the rest of his coffee, kicked off his state-issued slides, then stood up. The group started walking his way and niggas that stood around moved because they knew it was about to go down.

"Say, homie, yo' name Kilo?" the leader of the group said.

He sized the nigga up and saw that they were the same height and weight along with two other ones, but the one that stood in the back was tall but skinny.

"Yeah, why, what's good?" he asked as he got in fight mode.

"My homie Correy not feeling how you moving, so you know how that go."

Kilo laughed once he heard who had sent these lame-ass niggas his way. He didn't even say anything as he cocked back and hit the homeboy right in the chin. That put him to sleep instantly. His homeboys were shocked at their homie being knocked out, but Kilo was on ten and went for the one that was closest to him. He grabbed him by the shirt and slung him to the ground, then instantly began kicking him in the stomach. Kilos was amped up off of the coffee he had downed, so when the other nigga jumped on his back, he slung him off with ease. He continued to let ol' boy have it with his feet, connecting everywhere they pleased. By that time, everybody in the dayroom had begun to form a circle around them.

"PUSSY-ASS…NIGGA…SENT…YOU…WEAK-ASS…NIGGAS…MY…WAY? I'M… A… WHOLE… GANG-STA," he said as he kept stomping homeboy's head in.

The tall nigga finally snapped out of it and grabbed Kilo by the waist, then dunked him as hard as he could. As soon as he hit the ground, the tall nigga and the one he had slung off his back immediately started stomping him out. He started losing consciousness and before everything went black, he heard the turtles come in and lay everybody down.

***

Kilo woke up with a mean-ass headache, plus his whole body was sore from the beating he had gotten, so he just laid there. When he opened his eyes, he knew he was in SEG, and he laughed to himself. Correy had sent some weak-ass niggas his way, and even though he got on they ass, they had ended up getting the best of him. He sat up and noticed he had on the same dirty-ass clothes he got stomped out in. As soon as he was about to get up to call for the guard, his door was rolled open and Corporal Washington was there staring at him. He hadn't seen her since high school, and li'l momma's chocolate ass was looking good as fuck in her officer uniform.

"Kilo, yo' ass stay in some shit. You betta be lucky I know yo' ass, because if it is wasn't for me, yo' ass would be facing some more assault charges," she said as she was looking at him up and down.

"I appreciate that, li'l mama. You know I got you for looking out. I been in these bloody-ass clothes for a while. Can a nigga get a shower or what?"

"Boy, I just relieved the C.O. for a break, so you gon' have to wait for another hour," she said while looking up and down the run.

"Give me a pen and paper so I can write this number down for you so I can drop some bread off your way."

She pulled out her tablet and handed it to him along with a pen.

"This for the help and for you to get me in the tank with my brother, plus a little extra if you can get my two homies with us." He wrote down the number and a price.

When she saw the amount, she smiled and nodded her head in agreement. "How long you been locked up, since you got all this money to throw around?" she asked.

"A little over a month."

She looked down the run again, then stepped in his cell and grabbed his dick. She started massaging his dick through his pants and got the reaction she was looking for. When she found out that Kilo's ass was down here in SEG, she made her way to go see him. She paid her homegirl, who was the officer that was working the tank, to watch out for her. She had been crushing on Kilo since they were in middle school, and she finally had her chance to get with him. She knew this wouldn't take long, so she had to get in quick.

"Hurry up. Pull it out." She dropped to her knees.

Kilo was shocked but hurried up and whipped his already-hard dick out. When it popped out, her eyes got big at the size of it, and she knew it had been a while since he had a good nut because his balls was heavy as hell. She put that dick in her mouth as much as she could and tried to suck the life out of him.

"Shit, momma, eat that dick. DAMN!" Kilo said as he tried his hardest not to cum.

What she couldn't fit in her mouth she jacked off while she used a bunch of spit. She put his dick in the back of her throat, then looked up at him as he fucked her throat like it was a pussy. Before she knew it, he was filling her mouth up with nut. It was so much that it threatened to spill out, but she swallowed everything like a champ. She made sure she sucked every bit of nut he had left, then stuffed his still-hard dick back in his pants. She stood up and looked him in the eyes and knew he was satisfied.

"Make sure you stay out of trouble." She squeezed his dick one more time.

"You make sure you call that number, and it's more where that came from if you hold a nigga down while I'm here."

"Cool. I just might come back so I can feel that monsta in my stomach," she said, then walked off.

Kilo laughed as the door closed and he sat back on his bed. That was the last thing he expected to happen after an ass whooping like he just took. He just sat back enjoyed his nut and hoped that she came through for him again.

***

Quick and Savage had been waiting on the front porch for the U-Haul truck to pull up for about an hour or so now. They had copped another duplex three streets over from where Savage stayed. One side was to stash the load, and the other side would be used to cook and bag everything up. He had started recruiting niggas left and right along with bitches because he knew he was gon' need a team with what was coming his way. He spotted the U-Haul coming down the street and he waved it down and motioned for it to pull in the driveway that led to the back. When he noticed that there were two Mexican females inside, he smiled to himself because he liked the way Pablo did business. The police would never expect two women to be pushing drugs in a U-Haul up and down Highway 90.

He and Savage followed the U-Haul to the back and when he noticed that one of the girls was Pablo's daughter, he had a surprised but confused look on his face. He already knew she was pretty, but when he saw that slim, petite but curvy body she had, it made him look at her different. When the driver jumped out, he saw that she looked just as sexy as Jessica, but taller and thicker. She walked up to him, handed him the keys, then walked inside of their spot like she owned it.

"What's up, li'l mama, what you got goin' on?" Quick asked with a confused look.

"You have to take us back home. I figure we'll wait until y'all finish unloading the truck." She sat at the kitchen table across from her cousin.

Savage was smiling from ear to ear because he didn't mind kicking it with the two bad-ass bitches. Quick knew that he couldn't go there with Jessica because he knew Pablo would more than likely cut him off.

"Besides, you act like you don't want to kick it. I saw the way you was looking at me the other day. That's why I talked my papa into letting me and Laura bring you the load, so I can chill with you." She stepped in his face. She smelled good, so Quick couldn't help but inhale her perfume. She stared him in his eyes for a few seconds, then reached for the blunt that had already been filled with the best kush and lit it. She hit it, then passed it to him as she stood in front of him and watched him inhale the smoke like a pro. She smiled because she loved the way he looked. She always was attracted to black men, but never pursued one because she didn't know what her father would say. Once she saw Quick and Savage walk into their home, she knew she had to have him. Once she heard her father seal the business deal, she had begun to make her plans for her and Laura to make the drops to Quick.

Quick knew he could use Jessica to his advantage and decided to play along with her little game. "Li'l mama, you gon' fuck around and get what you looking for."

"Why you think I came?" She kissed him with as much tongue as she could give him. He kissed her back and gripped her ass cheeks while he pulled her in so she could get a feel of his dick.

"Damn! Papi! What is that?" she said in surprise.

"That's that grown man shit." He laughed as he moved from around her. He had forgot about Savage and Laura until he looked at the doorway and saw them lip-locked. He knew they both came to get some dick, but that had to wait because he had a truck to unload.

"Come on, Savage, let's get this shit over with before they make us forget the play." He walked out of the back door.

Savage followed along with Jessica and Laura. While they stood on the back porch, he and Savage lifted the U-Haul door up, and what they saw made their mouths drop. He looked back at Jessica and saw that she had a smile on her face. One side was stacked with fifty bricks of pure cocaine, and the other side had fifty pounds of kush. He spotted two trunks in the back and went to open them. He had a smile from ear to ear when he saw that they both were full to the top with all kinds of guns and ammo.

"My papa wants to talk to you," she said as she held up her phone.

He stepped out of the back of the truck and grabbed the phone.

"Mijo, I'm assuming you got what you needed," said Pablo.

"Hell yeah! Good looking out. I owe you big time."

"Usually there's no money to be made in war, but in order to start your empire, somebody's empire must die. Everything in that truck is enough to start yours. Be ruthless and rule with an iron fist," he said, then hung up.

He handed her phone back as he and Savage began to unload the truck. They both took off their shirts, then went straight for the guns. Once they carried both of the trunks off, they started for the weed, then the cocaine. It took them all of two hours because they would stop and smoke while Jessica and Laura lusted after their bodies.

"Li'l mama, do y'all got some homegirls that's tryna get paid?" Quick asked as he sat on the porch next to her.

"Yeah, why? What's up, papi?"

"I need somebody to help cook and bag shit up, and if you gon' ride with me, I'ma need your help."

"Papi, I'm about to get my papa to take you to another level. You think this is something? If you fuck with me, in a few more drops, I can get this doubled."

He pulled her onto his lap and kissed her just like the one she gave him earlier. He knew he decided to play her game for a reason and promised to play it out until it came out his way. No matter what it took, the streets would be his, and his grimy ways wouldn't let his mind rest as he plotted and plotted.

Ray Vinci

Chapter 5

Babygurl, Kiesha, Cassy, Sadie, and Ladie sat in the trap house off Skinnie's block dressed in all black as they loaded their guns. They all sat there quiet and smoked blunts back-to-back because they needed to prepare for the task ahead of them. This would be the first time they would ride out without Kilo and the rest of the squad, so they were nervous as fuck. Babygurl had wanted to ask Sean and his boys to ride with them, but they needed to do this on their own. She needed to let motherfuckas know that it wasn't shit sweet about them just because Kilo was locked up. She had called the number on the card that Special Agent Long had left and told him to find out where Quick was at.

He hit her back to let her know that at the moment, he was laying low, but that he had just opened a spot in the Rivieras on the Southeast side. There was a lot of money out that way, so she had to have it. She'd be damned if she let Quick show his face around the city like he didn't kidnap her and beat her half to death and be the cause of her squad being locked up. She tucked both of her 9mm guns and two extra extended clips in a drawstring Nike backpack and watched as her girls did the same.

"Y'all ready or what?" she asked while standing up.

She didn't have to ask because she knew that her girls were itching to get at Quick just as much as she was.

Her, Kiesha, and Cassy rode with each other while Ladie and Sadie followed behind them. She turned up her Cardi B as loud as it could go and zoned out the whole ride to the other side of town. She was remembering when she and Kilo would ride on any nigga who thought they couldn't get touched and it pissed her off because her ride or die wasn't riding with her.

It took them a little over fifteen minutes to get to the Rivieras and they parked at an abandoned house that was down the street. They grouped up to make sure everything was all good on their end.

"Nobody split up, because we need to be back here as fast as possible. Nobody in this spot lives, so murk everything that looks funny," Babygurl stressed to her squad.

All of them nodded in understanding as they jogged down the streets with their burners by their sides. She was told there were multiple traps inside of the apartments and she didn't know where to start, so she planned on busting at everything moving. They came in through the back and as soon as they rounded the corner, they spotted a group of niggas across from them. The group saw five people in black moving towards them and immediately pulled their straps. Before the group could up their guns in their direction, Baby-gurl was already sending shots their way. Three of them ran and ducked behind the building, but one stayed and got his body riddled with bullets. They got in rhythm as they made their way towards the apartment door. It might have been a while since they rode together, but it was like riding a bike. Sadie and Ladie rounded the corner and surprised all three of the niggas that were trying to hide behind the AC units. They let bullets spit from their guns as brains and bones painted the side of the apartment. Babygurl, Kiesha, and Cassy waited for them to meet back up and Cassy was the first one through the door with her guns blazing.

The two niggas sitting on the couch were the first to feel the heat as they got their chests filled with bullets. As the other four came in, they had to find something to hide behind as bullets came flying from the back rooms. They waited until the bullets stopped coming, then hurried up and rushed to the back. There were two bedrooms and a bathroom, so Babygurl and Kiesha took one and Sadie and Ladie took the other while Cassy took the bathroom. They cleared the apartment as they made their way to find the main trap. By the time they came out, niggas were waiting on them. They wasted no time emptying out the rest of their clips as body after body dropped.

They had to be careful with their bullets, because they didn't have too much. Before they moved on, they stopped at the park in the middle of the hood and reloaded their straps. Babygurl wasn't expecting it to be this much work, but they were gon' have to hurry up, because they knew the laws was on their way. All of them started moving at once with the motivation to kill. Babygurl spotted some niggas coming from an upstairs apartment in the corner and waited for them to come downstairs. As soon as the first one hit the last step, she put one in his head. He slumped down, and his homies thought twice as they came down and caught bullet after bullet. They quickly made their way up the stairs to the apartment, but to their surprise, there was nobody there but one dark-skinned female, a bunch of money, and some bricks of cocaine.

"Who's trap is this?" Babygurl asked with the strap pointed to her head.

The girl was crying and had snot running down her nose, so it was hard for her to speak. She had every right to be scared, because she was gon' get a bullet put in her shit if she didn't say what Babygurl wanted to hear.

"Quick's and Savage's! Please don't kill me. You can have everything!" she said while crying.

"Today is your lucky day. Tell that nigga Quick and whoeva the fuck that Savage nigga is that Babygurl coming," she said as they started sacking up a few bricks. They grabbed the two duffle bags full of money and made their way out of the door.

They heard sirens approaching the front of the apartments as they rushed and made their way to their whips. They loaded their trunks as they heard the sirens come to a halt and peeled back to the Eastside.

***

Quick had decided to kick it with Lexi today since it had been a while since they'd chilled. She was looking good as hell in her blue jean Polo one piece suit. She had on some black and white Retro 11s, and her curly hair hung loose down her back. Lovey had promised her she would watch the baby while she had some fun.

Lately, Lexi had really been regretting on how she handled the situation with Kilo. It seemed like she was missing him more and more every day and she wanted to find a way to get back right with him. She had already planned on going to visit him so he could see his daughter.

They pulled up to the Travel Inn behind the Valero off of Rittiman Road. Even though he was kicking it with Lexi, his phone was still jumping, so he needed a spot for the dope fiends and hustlas to pull up at. Plus he had to get some pussy because he was holding out on Jessica. It had been a week since he had got his first drop from Pablo, and everything was going good so far. He and his little team that Savage had put together had copped a few spots which were doing hellafied numbers. By the end of it all, he would be a millionaire, but only if he got ahold of that bitch and her squad.

They both hopped out of the car at the same time, but Quick let her go up the stairs in front of him. He watched her ass jiggle as she walked up the stairs in a slow sway and he knew they both had the same thing on their mind.

The room felt cool and comfortable as he sat down on the bed to relax. It seemed like he had been ripping and running the streets since Correy had been locked up. He really needed his nigga out right now at a time like this. Escobar showed him love but Pablo showing him way more love than Escobar could ever show. It seemed like at the thought of his homeboy, his phone rang. He looked at the screen but didn't know the number. He was going to ignore it but said fuck it and answered it anyway.

"Hello," he said through the phone.

"Yes, this is Ms. Walker, the lawyer that's working on Correy's case. He gave me this number so we could set up a meeting to discuss a payment plan."

Lexi heard a female voice on the phone and gave him a look that read "You got me fucked up." She stood up and unzipped her one-piece Polo suit and her titties popped right out due to her not having on a bra. His dick instantly got rock hard looking at those pretty-ass yellow titties.

"Huh? Yeah, just set the time and date." He leaned up while pulling down his Polo sweatpants and Polo boxers down in one motion.

"Well, we can meet up on Saturday if it's okay with you."

He said nothing because Lexi had already stuffed his dick in her mouth. His shit was too big to put all the way in her mouth, so she sucked half of it like she was making love to it.

"Hell yeah! Fuck!" he said softly, forgetting that he was on the phone.

She spit on his dick and began to jack him off fast as his dick stood tall and hard. She went back down and sucked and jacked like her life depended on it. She slobbered, gagged, and made slurping noises as her jaw began to hurt.

"Fuck, yeah, get that shit li'l mama!" he said loudly.

Ms. Walker said nothing as he laid back and enjoyed some of the best head game since Kiesha.

"Uh, sir, maybe I should call you back, because you sound busy," she said, hoping to catch his attention.

"Yeah, we can meet up Saturday…at…12:00 p.m. at…my house. Uhhh shit!" he tried to get out at Lexi swallowed every bit of nut that came out. "I'ma text you my address when we hang up."

He hung up as he saw Lexi come out of the one-piece. She not only didn't have on a bra, but she didn't have on panties either. She let him get an eye full, then pushed him back, climbed on top of the bed, and stood over his face. He was about to say something, but she squatted down and sat her leaking pussy right on his mouth. He stuck his tongue all the way out and let her grind slowly across it.

"Oh shit!" was all she could say. It had been a minute since she had a good nut, so she planned on taking advantage of this moment.

He gripped her soft ass cheeks to stop her movements so he could have his way. He sucked and slurped on her clit, which made her lean over to grip the headboard.

"Oh fuck, baby, yes!" she yelled. "I'm cum…cumming!"

She sat still on his face as she busted a hellafied nut that she had needed for weeks. He lifted her off of his face, then guided her to his dick. Once she sat on the head, she knew she would have her hands full. She sat down slowly until she felt she couldn't go down no more.

"Oh my God, daddy," she moaned as she bounced slowly on his monster. "You got a big-ass dick."

"Damn, this pussy good."

She had pussy juices leaking down his dick that dripped to his nuts. Just when she felt like she had taken all of his dick, he pushed in a few more inches. As soon as he had all twelve inches of his dick in her, she squirted all over his dick. She shook so hard that he had to grip her ass. He didn't wait for her to stop cumming and started slamming her down with force.

"Yo' li'l sexy ass gon' take all this dick."

"Yes, baby, give it all to me! Fuck!" she said while trying to get off of him at the same time.

She was about to cum again, but he flipped her on her back. He put both her legs over his shoulders and slammed every inch in her with long, slow strokes. He was hitting her stomach, so she scooted back some to get away from the pressure he was applying.

"Naw, don't run. Take this dick," he said as he followed her.

Despite all the pain she felt, she felt pleasure as well and began to cum again. He felt her cumming again and when she was done, he flipped her on all fours because he had to see that ass shake, plus he had to get his. He slid in slow because she felt tighter at this angle. He gave her slow strokes while he smacked her on her fat ass. He saw it jiggle and sped up, making her fall on her stomach. He landed right on top of her and the angle she was at gripped his dick and made him bust inside of her. They laid there for a few minutes until his phone rang,

He looked over and saw that it was Savage. Quick knew that it had to be an emergency because he had told him that he would be out of commission.

"What's up, homie? Talk to me," he said through the phone.

"Somebody hit our spots in the Rivieras and took everything," said Savage.

"What! Anybody know who did it?" he asked while sitting up.

"Everybody dead except one female."

"Where she at? Put her on the phone." He waited a few seconds, then listened as Savage told her to tell him everything.

"Hello," she said, sounding scared.

"Talk."

"A group full of females came through and killed everybody, then took everything. The only reason she left me alive was to tell you that she was coming."

"What she say her name was?"

"Babygurl."

"Cool. I'm on my way." He hung up. He was heated because Babygurl had struck first and he knew this was the beginning to an end. He just hoped it wasn't him to fall.

Ray Vinci

Chapter 6

Sean, his brother Li'l Tony, and his two cousins Rob and Baby Jay sat on the hood of an all-black Lincoln Aviator and a navy-blue AMG. Since they had been hustling with Babygurl, they had turned all the way up. They already had a little money from when they were in ATL, but now they were on a whole new level.

Babygurl had told them to meet her in the Landings so he could give her the money that they had for her. He was feeling Babygurl like a motherfucka, but the nigga Kilo had her head gone. She would always flirt and tease him, but she never folded. She was sexy, gangsta, and a hustla, so he made sure that every chance he got he would try to put her on his team. He knew that there was something off about her because she would always shoot slugs at him about not being ready for what they had going. He always shrugged it off and kept getting to the money.

The Landings was alive and woke as niggas and hoes walked around trying to find something to get into. Female was trying to holla and niggas were hating, but didn't say anything because this was Babygurl's spot. One thing she did do was make sure he was seen with her every time they went somewhere. He couldn't lie; Babygurl and her squad were bossed up. He could only imagine what type of status Kilo and his boys held in the streets.

As a group of hoes came around the corner and started bopping, he saw Babygurl's BMW followed by Sadie's Lexus coming through the gates. They quickly dismissed them because he knew Babygurl would trip, even though they weren't fucking. They pulled in next to them then jumped out while the girls were still standing there. Babygurl immediately walked up to Sean, then stood between his legs and kissed him on the lips.

"Hey daddy," she said, then looked at the females.

Her homegirls stood by his brother and cousins in a possessive way and looked at the girls the same way. All he could do was shake his head and smile because these hoes were crazy as hell.

"Girl, y'all asses is crazy," he said while sliding off the hood of his car.

"Why y'all always cock-blocking, but ain't never tryna come off no pussy?" Li'l Tony asked. He was feeling Cassy, but she never gave him no play.

"Y'all might start tripping and shit."

They all laughed at what Cassy said as they started high fiving each other.

"Shit, it's either that or y'all scared of dick," said Baby Jay while they laughed and dapped each other up.

Sadie walked up to him, then grabbed his dick and got as close to his face as possible. She liked what she felt and massaged it for a little bit until it got hard.

"All this dick, and you probably don't even know what to do with it."

Before she could back up, he gripped her ass and pulled her closer to him. "And all this ass and you probably can't take no dick." He then let her go roughly.

She liked that aggressive shit, so she had to back up quick, because he had her pussy wet.

Sean popped his trunk and pulled out a duffle bag as Babygurl popped hers so he could drop it in. The money was good, and he was loving every bit of it. He left the trunk open when he got inside of his car so he could turn up the Li'l Baby that was already in the deck. They had decided to kick it right where they were, so Ladie lit up kush blunts and passed them around. They were having fun as niggas and hoes started showing out. Hoes were popping their asses over niggas as niggas were going crazy. Everybody that was chilling in the parking lot was either a part of her team or trying to get with the team. She was kicking it with Kiesha when she noticed the same group of girls mugging them that they had checked earlier.

"What the fuck them bum-ass bitches staring at?" Kiesha asked.

"Fuck them hating-ass bitches," Babygurl said as she threw up the middle finger to them.

The girl that was bopping on Sean smirked, then texted something on her phone. Babygurl was about to go check that ass, but she and her group went inside of the apartment they were standing in front of.

"Scary-ass bitches," Babygurl said, then put her gun on the hood next to her. Being around Kilo kept her on point, so it was nothing to her to quickly bust her guns.

The crowds had calmed down a little bit, but as soon as the hood turned down, the money turned up. Dope boys and dope fiends were copping while they kicked it in the parking lot. The money was coming so fast that nobody saw the black Altima and the white van that crept through the front gate until it was too late. Savage was hanging out of the passenger side window of the Altima, letting loose the Uzi he was holding.

Everybody was quick but Rob and he got hit in the arm and leg multiple times. He screamed out in pain as Baby Jay pulled him behind the car. The side of the van slid open and four niggas hopped out busting as they dropped everybody that was still standing. Babygurl and Kiesha were behind the dumpster looking for their girls until they saw Cassy, Sadie, and Ladie hiding behind an apartment building with their guns out, looking at them. She smiled because she knew her squad was ready. She looked from behind the dumpster and when she saw Quick, her heart started beating fast. She stepped from behind the dumpster and let her finger molest the trigger of her 9mm. Quick ducked back inside of the Altima, barely getting out of the way of Babygurl's bullets. Sean, Li'l Tony, and Baby Jay was gunning at the four niggas who jumped out of the van while Sadie, Ladie and Cassy zoomed in on Savage. The only reason Savage didn't get his head popped off was because Quick smashed the gas while trying to run from Babygurl's and Kiesha's bullets. The van was left alone as all of them focused on killing whoever was left in it. Once the bullets had stopped and the smoke cleared, Sean and his boys put Rob in his car and smashed off to the hospital with his brother and cousin right behind him. Babygurl was mad because the nigga Quick almost caught her slipping, but because of them hating-ass bitches, she was on point. Now that she thought about it, she figured that bitch had texted Quick to let him know where she was.

Without saying anything, she walked towards the apartment that the girls went inside. It would be the last time anyone of those hoes ran their mouths.

***

Kilo had walked inside of the CK on the sixth floor of the county jail and saw Illy, Slugga, and Felony huddled under the stairs. Once they saw him come in, they rushed him and showed him some love.

"Damn, I feel like I ain't saw you niggas in years," said Kilo excitedly.

"What's the word on the streets?" Illy asked.

"Shit, I heard Babygurl and them got the streets on fire," said Felony.

"I know. Valerie came to see me the other day to let me know they were holding the streets down," said Slugga.

"Speaking of Valerie, I got her handling some business for me and I sent her to represent that bitch-ass nigga Correy. I'll be damned if I let that nigga get some time before I can smoke his bitch ass," said Kilo.

"Come on. My cell empty. Let's go put yo' shit up," said Illy as they walked upstairs to the corner cell.

It felt good to be around his squad again. Kilo just wished that they were out there with Babygurl and hers. Even though he knew she could handle her own, he still needed to be there. Word had already gotten back to him that she was kicking it with some nigga named Sean. He didn't know if she was fucking with the nigga like that, but she did give him a spot, so the nigga was at least hustling with her. He made a mental note to get some info about him. Now that he was situated with his squad, he was now waiting to see what Ms. Washington was gon' do.

"So what you got planned? I know you got something going on," Illy said as he sat next to his brother on the bottom bunk.

"Bianca got a judge to take my case for the mil I gave her. I'll be out in a couple of months. They want me to leave the state, but I ain't going nowhere no time soon," he said. "Her and Valerie working on y'all, so sit tight while our girls collect this money."

"What about them getting a new connect?"

"Shit, she got to do that on her own, because that nigga Escobar's rat ass is dead once I touch down. I got this corporal tryna make a move for us so we can live good in this bitch."

"I know you ain't talkin' about that thick-ass chocolate hoe that got us in here together," Illy said, surprised.

"Yeah, the li'l hoe feeling ya boy. She came through and hollered at me while I was in SEG. She even ate that dick."

"Stop lying, ugly-ass nigga."

"I ain't lying, just watch when that pack come in."

"I heard that nigga Correy put the thumb on you last week. Don't worry; I got an eye on that nigga anyways."

Kilo didn't say anything because every time he thought about it, it pissed him off more and more. He got up so they could go meet back up with Slugga and Felony so he could catch them up on what was going on.

When they made it downstairs, everybody was standing around the TV looking up. Kilo and Illy stood in the back as they watched the heli-cam show them the Landing Apartments. He saw a white van shot up and bodies being carried away. He had taken that spot from Correy, so he knew that Babygurl was the reason for the commotion. He smiled at his squad, and they smiled back because Babygurl, Kiesha, Cassy, Sadie, and Ladie had shit on lock. They just had to get out so they could be a part of the takeover.

Ray Vinci

Chapter 7

Valerie had stepped out of her red Camaro in a white skintight Yves St. Laurent one piece suit, and some white Christian Louboutin red bottom heels. She was on a mission for Kilo and planned to do whatever she had to do to get it done. She knew she was a bad white girl and loved black dudes with a passion. She was different from her cousin and loved what the street life had to offer but knew enough to stay on the light side. As she walked up the stairs, she felt nervous but she ignored it and got into her role. She knocked on the door and contemplated the shit she was about to do. As she heard the door open, she looked up at one of the finest chocolate niggas she'd ever seen. Once she got a good look at him, she knew that the job would be easy.

"Hi, I'm here about my client Correy," she said, sounding sexy.

She stood there looking sexy as ever while he looked her up and down like he wanted to eat her up. She thought about the day she had talked to him on the phone and her pussy instantly started to get wet. Once she saw him lick his lips, she smiled because she knew she had him locked up.

"Yeah, you can step in." He had to make himself snap away from her smile.

As he stepped to the side, she walked past him extra close while he got a good look at her ass. He had to admit that when he talked to li'l mama on the phone, he wasn't expecting her to look this damn good. He watched her as she sat down on the couch and looked around in awe. He knew his spot was cool and she probably was expecting some rundown-ass spot and a rundown-ass neighborhood. He made it a point to get himself a good crib to lay his head at that was away from all the drama. He sat on the recliner that was in the corner and looked at her.

"We can't do business with each other from way over there," she said while making eye contact with him. She had blue eyes and knew how to use them to her advantage.

He moved with the quickness, then sat so close that they were damn near touching.

"Okay. It should be pretty easy to get Mr. Correy out on probation due to the charges being fabricated by the leading detective," she said while flipping through the file folder that she had open on the coffee table.

He was looking at what was on the papers but didn't understand shit that was on them. All he needed to do was pay her fee so his boy could be back on the streets. He needed his homie, because shit was starting to get real, so he needed all he could get when it came to that gangsta shit.

"So how much is this gon' cost me? Because I don't understand none of this shit?" he asked.

"Well, for starters it's gon' cost you something to drink," she said.

"Li'l mama, I don't have no water up in here."

"I mean something harder than water, li'l daddy," she said while mocking him and smiling.

He got up then went to the kitchen to get something to sip on. He didn't know what type of shit she was on, but whatever it was, he was down for the play. While he was gone, she pulled out her cell phone and texted Bianca to let her know she was on the play. This wasn't the only thing she had to do to hold up this end of the plan. It was just the easy part.

Quick came back in with a bottle of Grey Goose and two glasses with ice in them. He poured up, and at the same time, pictured fucking the shit out of this little fine-ass white girl. He knew it was real when she grabbed one of the glasses and downed it in one gulp.

"So, about that price," he said, then sipped his drink.

"It's gon' cost you $20,000 for everything, and that's taking off $10,000 due to you being so fine," she replied in a sexy tone.

"I can do that. But what's up with all this?" he said while grabbing her and sitting her in his lap. "Damn, yo li'l white ass thick as fuck!"

His dick started rising as he rubbed all over her things. She felt his dick get hard and damn near jumped out of his lap. At the same time, her pussy got wet at all of the dick that she was feeling rise up on her. She started rubbing her ass against it just to tease him.

"Don't you have a girl handling all of this," she said, referring to his dick.

"Hell naw!"

"That ain't what I heard on the phone the other day, but from what I'm feeling, she had her hands full. I hope it's enough to go around," she said, then stood up. "I wish I had time to see what you working with, but I have another client to meet with."

All he could do was smile. He had forgotten all about how Lexi was sucking his dick when she called.

All she wanted to do was lock him in and just by what she did, she knew he would be calling her. She gathered her stuff and began to walk towards the door.

"When you ready to pay up, hit me up, cutie." She smiled then walked out the door, leaving him with a hard dick and a smile.

**

Lexi sat in the parking lot of Chacho's off of Perrin Bietle, contemplating what she was about to do. She felt like it was the right decision because the shit she was about to do, she didn't want her daughter nowhere around. She lit up a Newport because she was nervous as hell and felt like someone was watching her. She noticed the black Beamer pull into Chacho's parking lot and make its way towards where she was parked. Nobody knew about what she had planned so far, but now she was about to tell Bianca. Lexi watched as Bianca stepped out of the Beamer and even though she was pregnant, she was still bad as hell. She couldn't help but feel jealous because she still loved Kilo. Out of her, Babygurl, and Bianca, Bianca had to be the baddest one out of all of them. Bianca was a lawyer and had her shit together, which was one of the reasons Lexi chose to call her. Plus, she wanted Heaven to know her baby brother.

She got out and met Bianca halfway and they both just stood there staring at each other. They were the baddest bitches in the parking lot, and they both knew it without saying anything. Lexi, Bianca, and Heaven, who was barely walking, walked inside of the restaurant, then went straight to the back booth.

"I know you don't know me, but I really need this right now," said Lexi whole looking at Heaven.

"What do you plan on doing?" she asked.

"I need to help Kilo, and the only way I can do that is to set up Quick. I know Kilo and me could never be together again, but I need him to trust me, at least for our baby."

"So you want me to take care of your daughter while you try not to get yourself killed?" asked Bianca.

Before she could answer, the waitress came with their food. They said nothing as they dug in. Bianca was kind of glad to be taking Kilo's daughter in, but hated that it had to be under these circumstances. She knew that Kilo would be glad that she would be with his other child, and at the same time, he would be glad that Lexi was at least trying to right her wrong.

"So, what's the plan?" Bianca asked while sipping her Big Red soda.

"Once I leave here, I'm going to go see Kilo to let him know about what's going on. I have to play a close role to Quick so I can get all of the info out of him that I need."

"Okay, but we already got somebody on the job."

"Yeah, but right now I'm closest to him so I know it will be easier for me to get at him. Still, keep whoeva you got on him because I need all the help I can get with this nigga."

They had finished eating while plotting on how to get Quick. To both of their surprise, they got along well, which made them set up another lunch so they could kick it again. Once they were done, she kissed and hugged her baby and let her know that she loved her.

A few minutes later, she was driving down I-35 towards downtown. She was super nervous because she hadn't seen or talked to Kilo since the day of her sister's funeral. She knew she had fucked up by fucking with the enemy, but Kilo had no choice but to hear her out. No matter what it took she would gain his trust back. Even if he didn't want to hear her plan, she still would go through with it anyways. Lately, she hadn't been feeling the way Quick was acting. He was acting like he was better than everybody because he was getting a little money. She knew he was a pussy when it came to beefing with Kilo. She couldn't believe she let that nigga finesse her in the first place. It pissed her off even more just thinking about it, which made the plot even sweeter. She pulled up to the county jail and circled the block a couple of times until she found a good parking spot. Kilo would probably trip due to her not bringing his daughter, but he would have to understand. It took her twenty minutes to finally get in and get to the window she would be visiting Kilo in. While she waited, she pushed her nerves to the side and prepared for her baby daddy. Five minutes later, Kilo showed up, still looking like the boss he was even in his state-issued oranges.

"If I would've known it was yo' grimy ass, I would've refused. And why is you up here without my baby girl?" he asked with anger in his voice.

The look he had on his face would've killed her if looks could kill. It hurt her to see him look at her like that because he used to look at her with nothing but love.

"I know that you don't want to see me right now, but we really need to talk," she said with a cracked voice and tears in her eyes.

"We don't have shit to talk about. You chose your side, and it wasn't mine."

"I know I fucked up, but I need to make it up to you."

While she was talking, he stood up, getting ready to leave but she hit the glass with her fist to stop him.

"Please, baby, just listen to me!"

"If you ain't trying to give that nigga up, then we don't got shit to discuss."

"If you would listen, you would know what the fuck I'm tryna do!"

"You betta watch who the fuck you talkin' to! I'm not that bitch-ass nigga Quick. Now where is my daughter while you up here talkin out the side of yo' neck and shit?" he said aggressively to make sure he got his point across.

He knew when she stayed quiet that she still feared his gangsta. Lexi held her head down. A year ago, he would've felt bad for talking to her like that, but with the shit she pulled, if he could've touched her, he would've. Even with her eyes full of tears and her face beet red, she was still pretty as hell.

"Our baby is with Bianca."

She must've caught him off-guard because he was left speechless as she let her answer to his question hang in the air.

"And why is that?" he asked.

"Because what I got planned, I needed her to be in a safe place."

He stayed quiet and waited for her to continue.

"I plan on getting Quick for everything he owns, all the way down to his boxers. Once I got every penny to his name, your girls can come in and kill his bitch ass. Look, Kilo, I know that we will never be one again, but I need you in my life. Whateva it takes for you to trust me again, I will do it. Just name it and it's done," she said as she held eye contact with him.

What she said must've been music to his ears because he had a smile so big that it made her heartbeat for his.

"And what made you come to your senses since you did that stupid-ass shit?"

"I let that nigga get in my head, and now that nigga got some money, he be walking around like his shit don't stank. I know I fucked up in a major way, but now I got the chance to make it up. I just need for you to humble yo' girl Babygurl so we can make this shit happen."

"I got Babygurl. But what's your plan?" he asked curiously.

It took her less than five minutes to run her plan down to him. It wasn't much, but it was a start. He would take anything he could get right now. She was far from being forgiven, and he didn't know if that time would come, but for his baby, he would consider it. By the time the visit was over, they made plans for her to meet up with Babygurl and her squad. She would have to show her grimy ways to win them over, and she couldn't wait to prove she was just as grimy as most.

Chapter 8

The money was coming in so fast that they hardly had any time to chill and have fun. Today was Babygurl's birthday and they had been planning a big-ass birthday bash tonight at Bar 23. Even though it was her birthday, she didn't care because she felt like she had bigger problems. She was down to fifty bricks and no connect to re-up with. She didn't know how Kilo did it because this shit was giving her a big-ass headache, not to mention that nigga Quick. She hadn't seen or heard from him since that day he had come to hit them up in the Landings. She still couldn't believe they had let that nigga get away.

They were posted up in Sutton Oaks at Kiesha's trap, making ends meet hand over fist. It was jumping today, and they planned on getting every penny that came through this bitch. Babygurl was seeing racks on top of racks, but it wasn't the same without Kilo being out here. Niggas were trying them, but she and her girls weren't having that shit. They had been putting niggas and bitches down left and right along with the niggas that were already on the team before Kilo and them got locked up.

"Yo' ass ain't that deep into yo' thought to where you didn't hear shit I said," Kiesha said, snapping Babygurl out of her thoughts.

"My bad, bitch. I just got a lot on my mind right now."

"Let me find out it's that nigga Sean that got yo' mind fucked up," Cassey said, throwing her two cents in.

"Hell naw!"

"Girl, you need to give that nigga some sex, because you need some dick with yo' stressing ass," said Kiesha.

"I do need some dick, but I need a plug more than anything. We down to fifty bricks, which is about to be gone in a couple of days at the most. If we don't do something, we gon' be some broke bitches," she stressed to her squad.

"Why don't you hit up Escobar?"

"How about no, unless you want to be cellies in the county jail."

Sadie and Ladie stayed quiet the whole time but kept giving each other eye contact as Babygurl continued to stress her point. Babygurl caught the looks and had to say something.

"You two Asian bitches sure is quiet over there," she said. "Let me know what's on y'all mind."

They looked at each other one more time and Ladie gave Sadie a head nod. They didn't like talking about anything that had to do with their family, but if they didn't let them know they could help, they would be left on stuck. They hated to go to their daddy for anything, but they saw the worry in Babygurl's eyes, so they decided to play their part. By their daddy being married to their mom, he was automatically plugged in with their grandpa, who was a made man. Even though they barely went around their mom and dad, they knew he would help them in any way he could.

"I think we might have a way to solve all of our problems when it comes to finding a plug," Sadie said, breaking the silence.

"And y'all are just now bringing this up?" Babygurl asked.

"Yeah, because we hate to go to our daddy for anything. We have been out here grindin' on our own since we was fifteen, so we didn't have to go to him for nothing," Ladie chimed in. "But we're kind of in a bind, so we have no choice."

"Y'all mean to tell us y'all daddy got what we need to take shit over and y'all ain't said shit?"

"Yeah, but we need to try and find one on our own, because we didn't want daddy finding out what we had going on out here. I know you really need this, so consider this our birthday gift to you," said Sadie.

"If y'all wasn't my girls and it wasn't my birthday, I would whoop y'all's asses."

They all laughed because they loved each other to the death of it all. Babygurl also saw that they really didn't want to go to their daddy, so she understood their silence. She knew her girls loved her and was doing what was best for the squad. Without saying anything, she went to hug them both. Regardless, if they didn't get to connect with their pops, she would still love them to the moon and back.

"Alright, now that that's out of the way, let's hit up the mall so we can be the baddest bitches at the party," said Cassy.

"Yeah, let's just hope don't nobody try us, because we need to go at least one day without all of the street shit," Kiesha shot out.

"I know we have been all business lately. That's why I'm 'bout to get fucked up with plans of getting me some dick," said Babygurl.

"You damn right!" Sadie shouted as they all gave each other high fives.

They went inside of the trap to get themselves together which took 30 minutes due to them smoking. Babygurl, Kiesha, and Cassy rode in Babygurl's BMW while Sadie and Ladie rode in Ladie's brand-new Lincoln Aviator. Even though they hadn't been having fun, they had spent a little money on themselves.

Sadie and Ladie pulled out of Sutton Oaks first with Babygurl right behind them. They were always seen five deep due to most females hating or just plain stupid to try them. Most of the females they put down tried to get in their immediate circle, but they always cut that shit short. The only people they did let close to them were Sean and his boys. As soon as she was about to plug up her phone to put some music on, her phone vibrated. She looked at the screen and saw that it was a county jail number and knew that it was Kilo.

"Hey daddy!" she said excitedly with a big-ass smile on her face.

"What's good, Babygurl? Happy birthday, li'l momma," he said from the other end. "How you holding up out there?"

"I'm good right now, and my girls hold it down for the squad."

"What about that bitch nigga?"

"I just hit him up a couple of days ago when he slid through poppin' that hot shit our way. Other than, that he in hiding," she said in code the best way she could. She knew that they were probably listening to all of Kilo's calls, so she had to be careful about what she said. It felt like it had been a long time since she last talked to Kilo, so she was happy as hell just to hear his voice. She kept his books laced to the fullest, and every time he sent someone her way, she made sure she handled whatever he needed handled.

"Say, li'l momma, I'm about to shoot Lexi your way on some shit that's gon' help you out."

"I don't need that bitch's help for shit, so she can stay her scary ass wherever she at!"

"Calm yo' crazy ass down. She is our other way to get to Quick. She gon' find where his spots at so you can hit his pockets," said Kilo calmly.

"I can hit his pockets on my own. I don't need no stank-ass bitch! Me and my bitches got this shit chill!" she said with anger in her voice.

He could tell she was mad because she sounded like a Mexican when she was tripping. He chuckled to himself because he got the response he knew he was about to get. If she would have came out of the side of her neck any other way, he would've thought she had gotten soft on him. He also chuckled because he knew if she was in his presence, she wouldn't even talk stupid.

"Girl, you got me fucked up with the way you poppin' that hot shit. I told you she gon' play her part, and that's what the fuck gon' happen. You don't even have to deal with her. She just gon' hit Bianca, and from there, Bianca gon' hit you up," he said to her and he knew she got her shit together. He hated talking to her like that, but that was the only way to get through to her crazy ass.

"Alright, but if that bitch get out of pocket, I won't hesitate to smoke her ass."

"Don't worry, li'l momma cool. I'ma let you get on with your day. Have fun and tell the girls we said what up," he said, then hung up.

It seemed like as soon as she hung up, the police car behind her hit his lights. When they saw the lights, they didn't panic. They all tucked the burners they had under the seats as Babygurl pulled over. All three of them had been through this shit, so it was nothing new to them. Babygurl was just glad that Sadie and Ladie were good. Once she looked in the mirror and saw Detective Stronbone, all she could do was laugh.

"Well, well, well, if it isn't Mrs. Kilo herself. I've been looking all over for y'all for a couple of months. Now can you tell me why y'all's names are ringing like church bells in these streets of San Antonio?" he said with a smirk on his face.

"Don't know what you talkin' about, Mr. Officer," she said as Kiesha and Cassy stayed quiet.

"Just like Kilo. But just like I got his black ass, I'ma get yo' little sexy ass. I just stopped you to let you know that. I'm investigating y'all, so prepare for your downfall, Mrs. Kilo," he said, then walked away laughing.

She was pissed off, so she smashed off without even turning up the radio. She kept looking in the rearview mirror to see if he was still following her. She couldn't believe that she didn't notice his cop ass following her from the jump. She calmed herself down because she refused to let anything fuck up her day.

She made her way downtown so she could get herself together for her birthday. One thing she did know was that she was gon' be watching for that bitch-ass white boy.

***

Shit had been moving kind of slow lately due to Quick closing down two of his best spots and his count house. He didn't want to take a chance of Babygurl hitting him again, so he had to close shop for a couple of days. He had been tucked low since the day he tried to ride down on her in the Landings. He wasn't expecting them niggas to be with her, whoever the fuck they were. He had heard that she was turning motherfuckers up, but he thought that was just on a hustling tip. The niggas that were with them didn't hesitate to bust back when they came through.

Tonight, he and his team would step out and show out. He has been hustling every day, so in addition to his $200,000, he was now sitting on $450,000. Pablo had him eating good, but Babygurl was in his way. He had visions of him and his team being millionaires by the time Correy stepped out. He would make sure his homie was straight once he came home because when he was down Correy didn't hesitate to pick him up. That was one of the reasons he looked out for Savage. He and Savage had plans to lock down the VIP section of Bar 23 for their team because they were going hard as a motherfucka. They needed two bad-ass bitches on their arms, so they planned to bring Jessica and Laura. He just hoped nothing popped off while they were with them. He was already sneaking around with her behind Pablo's back.

He had just finished rolling the blunt when he heard Savage system beating down the block. Now that he was here, he was only waiting on Jessica and Laura.

"I'm telling you, homie, I'm about to turn up once we get in that bitch," Li'l Nut said as he popped two mollies.

"Nigga, you ain't gon' do shit. As soon as one of them hoes try to holla, you gon' nut up wit' yo' scary ass." Gee said as everybody started laughing.

"Man, fuck you," he said, salty.

Savage walked in dressed in Gucci from head to toe with ice dripping from his neck, ears, wrists, and fingers. Before he could say something, somebody knocked on the door and all of them came off of their hips with the quickness. Quick had come from the kitchen with an all-black Mossberg pump in both his hands, ready to buck at whoever was on the other side of his door. He signaled for Savage to open the door while all seven of them aimed their burners at the same time. When he opened it, two of the sexiest Mexican girls came in looking like the money they were both worth.

"Damn, papi, you even more sexy with that Mossberg along with these niggas. But can y'all quit pointing them guns at us? Damn," Jessica said while sounding like she was just brought over from Mexico.

She was dressed in a skintight red Fendi dress with some all black Fendi heels that made her ass seem fatter than it already was. Her curly hair was pulled back in a ponytail to show off her pretty facial features, but also to show off every piece of bling that was glossing from her body. Laura had on a blue Louis Vuitton dress that buttoned up the front with some black Alexander McQueen shoes and some iced-out jewelry. Her hair was cut in a bob, which looked good against her white-complexioned skin, whereas Jessica was dark.

"My bad, li'l momma. Shit just been crazy lately," he said as his team of young killas put their guns away. "Damn, yo li'l slim ass lookin' sexy as hell. Come show a nigga some love."

She got excited as she gave him a kiss and a hug. "You smell just as good as you look," she said as she inhaled his cologne.

"You smell good ya damn self." Laura showed Savage the same kind of love as their li'l homies looked on. They both matched their fly, so they couldn't help but admire their bossmen.

"Don't worry, we got some girls already posted in VIP for y'all. Y'all rolling with some boss bitches, so trust, we know how our boss niggas' homies needed something to hold on to for the night."

They walked outside to get in their cars and made their way to Bar 23 with plans to show out.

***

When Quick pulled up to the club, cars were lined up down the street. He didn't know the club would be this packed, which made him even more excited to get in. Jessica sat in the passenger seat, just as excited as Quick was. She had never been out with these kinds of people and was fascinated with their lifestyle. Savage and Laura were in the backseat blowing sticks of that gas while his team followed behind closely. Evidently, it was a birthday bash and the birthday girl came out to stunt. He didn't know who she was, but he planned on outdoing her anyway. He didn't give a fuck about anybody that wasn't with his get down, so fuck everything else.

They parked on the side of the club, but close to the door just in case he had to make a quick escape. He went straight through the door as he had paid for his whole team and a little extra just so they could bring their straps.

Once inside, they heard Li'l Baby bustin' through the speakers while hoes and niggas were dancing and having fun. This bitch was packed from wall to wall, so he hurried up and made his way towards VIP. They saw the group of females that Jessica mentioned earlier. When they stepped in, the five li'l homies chose up and sat next to the females. Bottles instantly started popping as everybody poured up the Grey Goose that was sitting on ice. Jessica found her a spot to sit down, which was on Quick's lap. Her Fendi dress rose up over her thighs as she sat facing the dance floor. She heard Cardi B bust through the speakers and started popping her ass to the beat on Quick's lap. His dick got hard so fast that it caught her by surprise when she felt all that meat pop up against her ass cheeks.

He had just started to relax and have fun until he looked across the way into the other VIP section and saw Babygurl looking dead at him. Her stare was so deadly that it made him uncomfortable.

"Baby, we gon' go to the ladies' room," she said as she and her homegirl walked out of the booth.

"Say, Savage, there go them hoes over there with them bitch-ass niggas."

"Let's go get at them weak-ass hoes right now then," said Savage while looking the way Quick was looking at.

They both came to the conclusion that she was the reason the club was on smash. If she was the reason the club was on smash, that meant half of the club was her squad. He wanted so bad to send bullets, their way but he couldn't risk putting Jessica and Laura in danger.

"Naw, homie, we got the plug's daughter and niece with us. If anything happens to them, we out of there," he explained.

His young killas weren't trying to hear none of what he was talking about, so he had to calm their asses down. Savage understood, so he let it go. She must've known at the moment he didn't want no smoke, so she threw up two gun signs with a smirk on her face and at the same time, all seven of them threw theirs up. He couldn't lie; Babygurl and them bitches was bad as hell, and for some reason, he had no choice but to respect her gangsta. The only reason he was beefing with her was because of Correy, plus that grimy-ass bitch Kiesha. He was so into his thoughts and staring at the other section that he didn't even see the girls show back up.

She sat right back on his lap, but this time facing him. Her dress raised up slightly above her ass cheeks, which left the bottom exposed. He gripped them as she sucked on his neck while he continued to stare at Babygurl.

"Whateva is on your mind, I hope this pussy can take your mind off of it," she whispered in his ear. His mind was saying fuck getting some pussy, but his dick had other thoughts. The slower she grinded, the harder his dick got. When she realized that he was focused somewhere else and followed his gaze, she knew he wasn't feeling any of the females over there because his mug was so mean that it scared her.

"Who is that hoe, papi?" she asked him with concern in her voice.

He didn't answer her because Babygurl, Kiesha, and Sean were walking up to the VIP booth.

"You gots to be one crazy-ass bitch to roll up on me just three deep," he said.

"First off, crazy is only half of what you done seen. Insane is the part you don't wanna see. Second, I ain't scared of you, these niggas or none of these stank-ass hoes." She mugged every hoe that was there. Kiesha was right by her side mugging every bitch in sight. "Third, I bought the club so every nigga in this bitch work for me."

"And I see you brought this weak-ass nigga with you. I know this nigga ain't even half of what Kilo is, and you kickin' it with him and you got this bitch with you," he said, then smirked.

"Nigga, I didn't come to hold no conversation with you. I just came to give you one more chance to burn up out of my city."

"How about I give you a chance to get out of my city?"

"Alright, I gave you a chance," she said, then walked off with Kiesha and Sean right behind her.

Sean stopped and turned around. "Nigga, I'll clap yo' stupid ass any day. Don't ever compare me to no nigga, 'cause my gangsta just as lethal as yours, pussy."

Babygurl was glad that he said something to him, because she didn't want to question his get down when it came time to handle his business.

Quick was hot, along with his goons. He didn't do anything because he was outnumbered, so he let her slick-ass comment slide off of his back.

"Don't worry, papi. Just fuck with me and I'll make sure you run not only San Antonio, but everything outside of it."

He sat back and enjoyed what little of the night he had left. He eyed the other VIP booth with murder in his vision.

Chapter 9

After they left the club, everybody made plans to kick it at Sean's penthouse for the night. They chose his spot because it was off of Broadway, so motherfuckas never came that far out, plus nobody but this circle knew about this spot. Once they got settled, smoke instantly filled the air from the blunts of purp that were being passed around. Sean sat in the recliner that sat facing the whole room. He and Babygurl made eye contact, and it seemed like she had something on her mind. He knew she had something on her mind because he sure as hell did. He was beefing with a nigga he didn't even know and damn sure didn't know why, and he was tired of getting compared to whoever this nigga Kilo was.

"You got something on yo' mind?" Babygurl asked due to the slight mug on his face.

"When you gon' tell me about why you beefin' with this nigga? This is the second time I done seen the nigga, and each time it's been some bullshit. And who the fuck is this nigga Kilo? Because every time I go around somebody you know, they bring his name up." He hit the blunt while he waited on her reply.

"Alright, I guess I do owe you an explanation. First off, Kilo is my ride or die. He started this shit from the ground until him and the rest of the niggas in the squad got knocked. As far as this nigga Quick…"

She explained everything to him from Rico all the way til she got kidnapped. They all listened and understood why she wanted the nigga dead. The only reason she told him everything was because she was really starting to grow feelings for him. She hadn't had feelings for a nigga since Kilo, but there was something about Sean and his gangsta that made her feel some type of way. Without saying anything, he grabbed his cup of Goose off the table and the already-lit blunt that was in the ashtray then went to the back room. He had to let everything that Babygurl just told him settle on his brain. It was a lot to process, but he knew that everything that was said and done had to remembered for right now. He took his shirt off, then sat on the edge of the bed as his sipped his drink. He hit the Sweet, then let the smoke settle in his lungs.

He was so deep in thought that he never heard the room door open. He looked up and noticed Babygurl standing with her back against the door. He stared at her and couldn't help but notice how bad this Mexican bitch was. He was falling for li'l mama, which was wrong due to the position he was in.

She started walking his way, and he knew exactly what she had on her mind. He'd been waiting on this moment since the first time he saw her li'l short thick ass. She said nothing as she straddled his lap. He raised her Christian Dior dress over her head and his dick got hard as steel once he saw that she had nothing on underneath. She pushed him back, and with just her Dior heels on, hopped on his face. Sean wasted no time putting his tongue in overdrive as he gripped her soft ass cheeks.

"Oh! My! Shit!" she moaned loudly as she grinded on his tongue.

He sucked on her clit with the intention of draining every drop of her juice that he could get.

"Fuck, baby, eat…this…pussy. I'm about to cum!"

Even though she was shaking off the nut she was having, he kept sucking, slurping and locking her pussy in figure 8's until he had her busting again. She couldn't take anymore, so she got up, then went straight for his B.B. Simon belt buckle. Once she got it unbuckled, she pulled his pants and Polo boxers down all at once. His dick popped out, hard and ready as ever. She loved what she was seeing as she played with it a little and slowly jacked his eight inches.

"Quit teasing a nigga and handle ya business, li'l mama," he told her as he looked own on all her beauty,

She chuckled, then deep throated him in one motion. Her mouth was so warm, it felt like she was heating up his whole body. She was sucking the shit out of his dick with more spit than he thought one person could produce. Li'l mama's head game was on 10, because he felt himself wanting to run.

"Damn, li'l mama, eat that dick. Oh shit! Hell yeah!" he said while in pleasure.

"Damn, you got a lot of dick, baby. I'm finna show you what I can do with this big motherfucka."

She spit on it, then jacked him off with both of her hands with speed and finesse. She went right back to work on that dick as she repeatedly stabbed the back of her throat with it. She slurped, gagged, and spit, trying to get him to nut. It didn't take much longer for him to start busting down her throat. She swallowed every drop like a champ and kept on sucking to get everything that she worked hard to get. His dick was still hard, so she climbed on top and slid down slowly due to him being so big.

"Uh, fuck, baby, you too damn big!" she said as she slid down slow. She bounced on it as soon as she got halfway because she was full. "Oh! Fuck!" She nutted all down his dick and it dripped down his big balls. It had been a minute since she had any dick, so she busted ASAP. Her pussy was so slick that once he grabbed her ass cheeks and guided her down, she went all the way down with ease. He wasn't about to play no games with this pussy, so he pumped in her with long strokes. She tried to come off his dick, but he had a good grip on her ass.

"Oh! Fuck! It's too much!" she yelled as she tried to get away. "Yesss! Yes!"

"Damn! Who pussy is this!"

"Yours, daddy!" was all she could get out because he was flipping her on her back.

Without taking his dick out, he put her legs over his shoulder and pounded her pussy out.

"Unh! You…fuckin'…the…shit!" She was busting a nut because he was deep in her stomach. She was running from the dick, but he was right with her.

"Naw, don't run. Take this dick," he said as he went to work on her juice box. He wanted to get his nut, but he had to hit that ass from the back, so he flipped her over.

She put her face in the bed and her ass in the air, which she instantly regretted as soon as he went back in.

"Damn, this pussy good, li'l mama."

She had her face in the sheets, so all you heard was moans and the smacks of their skin. Her ass was jiggling out of control and that made him bust all in her guts. They were both tired, so as soon as they finished, they smoked a Sweet of purp then fell into a deep sleep.

***

They had to meet up with Pablo to drop off the money from the last shipment and for this drop they were about to pick up. Pablo wanted to meet him in person to see how he was doing. Even though he knew that Pablo knew about Babygurl, he wasn't about to tell him. As far as business went, he was doing numbers. He was easily making $100,000 a day that he had to split with Savage and his young killas. He had half of the city on lock, but Babygurl was in his way. Word on the streets was that her dope supply was running low, which was good because he was planning to move on one of her spots on the east side. Savage had come out with the two duffle bags and a backpack full of money. Altogether, it was $350,000.

"Shit, I'm ready whenever you ready," Savage said as he tossed one bag by his feet and kept one along with the backpack.

"Let's ride then, gangsta," said Quick while he tucked his burna, then picked up the bag.

"I still don't understand why this nigga want to do a drop at his main crib," said Savage.

"Shit, me neither, but fuck it. As long as homie got my pockets right, then I'm good. Real talk."

They threw money in the newly-copped G wagon that Savage had just got off of the lot, then waited for two of their best shooters to jump in their whips so they could follow. Once everything was situated, they peeled off toward the Northside. He turned up his Moneybagg Yo, lit up a Sweet, and relaxed as he sat in the passenger seat. He was snapped out of his thoughts minutes later when his homie turned the music down.

"I got a serious-ass question," said Savage.

"Shoot." He hit the blunt a few times, then passed it to Savage. "This li'l Mexican bitch a problem for us, why don't we just smoke her li'l bad ass?"

"I wish it was that easy, because I would've been popped li'l mama a long time ago," he said. "This li'l bitch and them hoes is some straight-up gangstas. They were bred by some gangstas that's probably about to get out real soon. I figure if I wait until Kilo and his squad get out, we can get all of them at once instead of two separate squads."

Savage nodded his head because it did make a little sense. He figured they would keep stacking money and keep recruiting killas to ride with them. When Savage looked at Quick, he saw that he was smiling at his phone.

"Nigga, why you keep cheesing so hard?"

"I got this li'l bad-ass white hoe that's trying to link up with a nigga."

"Oh yeah? See if she got somebody for me."

"I got you, but first let me do me."

For the rest of the way, they smoked and listened to music, not knowing that two cars behind them, somebody was lurking.

Ray Vinci

Chapter 10

It had been a week since she had last seen Quick's bitch ass, but she wasn't stunting that nigga right now because she had an important meeting to go to. She was going to tell Sean and his boys to roll with her, but something was telling her not to. It was cool though, because she had her girls with her. They were down to ten bricks, so this meeting was mandatory. Quick was already moving in on her spots because her work was running out, but hopefully that would stop after they met Sadie and Ladie's pops. Usually Kiesha and Cassy rode with Babygurl, but today, Sadie rode shotgun while Ladie rode in the back. The car was filled with loud smoke while City Girls blasted through the speakers. Babygurl reached over to turn the music down to break the silence.

"I just want to thank y'all for coming through for the squad," said Babygurl.

"Don't start that sensitive-ass shit. We just playing our part. Now my daddy is more than likely about to get in our asses because this was the life he was tryin' to keep us from. One thing I do know is that he is about to take us to a level that none of us expected to be on," explained Sadie.

"Whateva level he about to put us on, trust and believe that we gon' live up to it. I got a team of bad-ass bitches that can't be fucked with," she said, then hit the loud. "As long as we got each other's backs, we'll be unstoppable."

"Y'all are some bad-ass bitches," Ladie said from the backseat.

They all busted out laughing at the comment as they pulled up to Canyon Lake. These houses was big as fuck, so once Babygurl saw them, her mouth dropped open. She was raised on the Eastside all of her life and had never seen houses this big. As she drove up the driveway, she knew that she was about to elevate her squad to a whole new level. She was nervous as hell along with Sadie and Ladie because she didn't know what to expect.

They pulled up to the gate and were buzzed in immediately due to them being waited on. They stopped in front of the door and were met by a big bald black man and a tiny Asian. Both of them were strapped with Dracos along with the other multiple guards that roamed the property.

"This is the type of shit I'm talkin' 'bout," Babygurl said to herself.

Once they stepped on the porch, a tall slim Asian woman came out speaking Japanese. Sadie and Ladie spoke back to her in the same language and Babygurl looked at them sideways.

"You bitches speak Japanese? Hell naw! Y'all just full of surprises."

Before Sadie or Ladie could speak up, the lady said something.

"I'm sorry. I'm Kim Li. I'm their mother," she said in English.

"Hi, I'm Babygurl, and I must say, you are very beautiful." She had to admit she saw where they got their looks from, but they had to have got their asses from their daddy's side because momma was flat in the back.

"Thank you, and you are beautiful as well. Come. Tree is waiting for you'll." She turned to walk inside.

Once they got inside, Babygurl was in awe because they had a mixture of a Black culture and an Asian culture. The hallway was long with tall marble pillars connected to high ceilings. Along the walls were African statues as well as Asian statues. Her heels clicked against the black and white tile, which looked spotless. Kim Li led them to a room with a long table that was filled with all kinds of delicious-looking food.

At the table sat a tall caramel-skinned man that looked like he came straight out of the hood. He was dressed in some blue fitted Polo jeans, a red and white striped Polo collar shirt, and some all-white Polo loafers. His attire was complete with jewelry that draped his neck, ears, and wrists. His fade was on point, plus the smile he had showed off the deep dimples on his face. He looked young, but Babygurl knew better. He whispered something to the butler, then looked up as the butler walked off. He waved them over as the twins went to show their pops some love.

"Daddy, this is Babygurl, the one I was telling you about." Sadie said as they all took seats. It just so happened that she ended up sitting across from him.

"What's up, li'l mama? I'm Tree," he said, giving her a head nod.

"What's up?"

"So my babies tell me that y'all have a problem," he said as the butler came in to make their plates.

"Yeah, we do, but to be honest with you, I'm not too good at this because I'm used to my nigga Kilo handling this type of shit. What I do know is I got a team. The streets is mine and I got a whole bunch of money." She ate a piece of steak.

He laughed because he respected her honesty. "I've been trying to keep the twins from following in my footsteps, but I see that didn't work. Since I feel where you coming from and they begged me to help y'all out, I think we can make something work." He sipped the brown liquor that was in his glass.

The twins looked at Babygurl with smiles the size of the Kool Aid man.

"Now, Sadie and Ladie, y'all cousin Twan is trying to step his game up, so I need y'all to give him a spot."

"I'll make sure he's good." Babygurl said because she saw the way they looked like they didn't like what was said, plus she needed to let him know that she was in charge. Apparently, he understood because he gave her a look of approval like he was testing her.

"Now the big question is, what is this going to run us?" she asked.

"Alright, first load's on me. Second load gon' run you ten apiece. The load gon' consist of half coke and half heroine. I'ma even give you a team of gangstas to handle the li'l beef I'm hearing about in the streets. Don't look surprised. I grew up on the Eastside, so I still got my ears to the street, li'l mama," he said with a slight smile.

"Shit sounds good to me."

After they sealed the deal on their new business arrangement, he and Babygurl got to know each other through loud blunts and brandy. She was glad that shit went her way, and they exchanged info to drop the load off with plans to make the drops.

Five hours later, they were headed back to meet up with the rest of the crew to let them know that all was good and that they were back in business.

***

Quick knew Babygurl had thought shit was sweet because he didn't clap back from the little stunt she had pulled last week. He had been plotting for a week straight on how he was gon' get back at her and was finally about to hit one of her spots. He was hearing through the streets that Babygurl was low on work, so his plan was to take her down for it. Quick had one of his goons sit on Kilo's old spot off of Martin L. King and had struck gold. He knew that she was stashing her work somewhere and decided to check out the old trap that sat on Skinnie's block. Once his goon had told him what he knew, he had instantly put a plan together to hit it. He was hoping that by hitting her little stash spot it would hurt her hustle for a little bit. Quick needed the streets to win this little war he had going on with Babygurl, and he was willing to be the grimiest nigga in San Antonio to do it.

He was interrupted from his thoughts by Savage handing him a blunt of kush.

"Damn, my nigga you gon' like that?" I been tryna pass you this Sweet for like two minutes," said Savage as he passed him the blunt.

"I'm good, my nigga. I wish this nigga Slim would hurry his ass up."

They had been watching for over two hours for Slim to call and let them know they were good to hit the spot. As if on cue, Quick's phone rang and he knew it was Slim, so he picked up automatically.

"Tell me something good, li'l homie," he said through the phone as he hit the Sweet.

"Them hoes gone, but it's like four niggas in the house and two that's standing outside at all times," said Slim.

"We on our way. We like minutes away." He hung up the phone as he pulled out into traffic.

"That was Slim, and he said them hoes gone, but it's at least six niggas there, so we air them niggas out then take everything in that bitch," Quick said.

"Cool."

It took them no time to get there because they were already a few blocks away. Once Savage got to Skinnie's block, he circled it two times to make sure everything was all good. He parked the car down the street but made sure to keep it running just in case shit got too real. They got out and walked coolly down the street because they saw the two niggas that were on the front porch. Quick instantly noticed that those were two of the niggas that were at the club with Babygurl. His blood instantly began to boil as he remembered how the nigga by her side had disrespected him. Once they were a few feet away, he pulled his heata out and began busting toward the niggas on the porch. As soon as the niggas on the porch heard the shots, they dove to the ground and crawled to the side. Savage was right on the side of Quick, letting his burna talk as they both put holes in the house. As they got closer, bullets from the AK 47 that was hanging out of the front window sprayed the side of the car that they ducked behind.

"As soon as he stop shootin', that nigga gotta go!" Quick yelled over the gunshots.

When he finished his sentence, the bullets stopped and Savage jumped up and lit up the window. He knew he popped whoever it was because the AK dropped outside of the window. They both advanced quickly on the house with murder on their mind. Savage had kicked the door in just as Slim had pulled to a stop right in front of the house. As soon as they stepped inside, shots rang out, which made them jump back out. Slim being the gangsta he was pulled out both of his black 9mm guns, stepped through the doorway, and let off shot after shot. He heard two bodies drop, so he felt like the coast was clear. Quick and Savage walked in behind him and both were sprayed in the face with blood and brain matter as Slim's head exploded from the bullet that went through his forehead.

Quick sent wild shots the way the bullet had come from. He had started panicking because it was only a matter of time before niggas came to help. There were three left, so he needed to smoke them so he could get what he came for and burn. Babygurl kept a squad of gangstas, so he knew he had to come with it every time. He heard movement in the back, so he crept back that way slowly. He spotted a nigga's head peeping around the corner and all it took was a few shots to the head. They both went their separate ways inside of the house to see what they could find.

Quick, already knowing the layout of the house, went straight to the room where Kilo used to put the bricks. When he opened the door, all he saw was ten bricks stacked in the far corner. He smiled because he knew this would hurt Babygurl and hopefully shut her out of the game. He was so into his thoughts that he forgot that Savage was in the other room until he heard shots coming from the living room. When he made his way back up front, he saw Savage standing over one of the niggas that was posted up on the porch.

"Where the other one?" asked Quick.

"Bitch-ass nigga got away."

"Let's go before these niggas get to trippin'."

Quick ran back to the back, loaded up the ten bricks, and made his way back up front. Once Savage made it back with a sack of money, it took them no time to make it back to their whip, then burned off across town.

Chapter 11

Babygurl, Kiesha, Cassy, Sadie, Ladie, Sean, and his little crew were waiting on their first drop. She had just copped a spot in the back of the Goldfield Apartments off of Rittiman Road because she needed a new stash house. She gave Tree the address and they made plans for every drop to make its way there. He hadn't told her how much was on its way, but she knew it was big. Hopefully Tree would put her on a level that would push Quick's along with Correy's asses off of the map.

Her phone rang, snapping her out of her thoughts, which made her look up to see a black F-250 with the back end of a truck hooked to it. She was all smiles as she answered her phone without even looking at the screen.

"Talk to me," she said through the phone as she waved the truck to where she was.

"Babygurl, they just hit the spot for the last of what we had left! They smoked everybody that was there. I just so happened to get away!" he said in a hurry.

She had to look at her phone at first to see who it was, but once the voice registered in her head, her mind started racing a million miles an hour. "Who?" was all she could say.

"Quick."

"Alright, I'm in Goldfield. Come my way so we can talk," she said, then hung up.

The F-250 pulled up when she hung up, but her eyes were on her squad. They could tell she was mad as hell, so they decided not to even ask. She wanted to make sure everything went well before she told them anything.

When the driver jumped out, Sadie and Ladie ran to their big cousin and gave him a hug. It had been a long time since they saw Twan, so they were happy to see him.

"Damn, who is this fine-ass nigga?" Cassy asked.

"I'm Twan." He looked the whole squad over, even Sean and his little team.

Before anybody could say something else, the back end of the truck door slid up and four niggas jumped out with Dracos. All in one movement, Babygurl, Kiesha, and Cassy pulled their straps and were ready to shoot anyone of them niggas.

"Naw, li'l mama, they with me and I'm their big cousin," Twan said as he hugged Sadie and Ladie.

"Well why the fuck they hop out with those big-ass guns? Almost got they stupid asses clapped," she said as they put their guns away.

All he could do was laugh because he had heard so much about the infamous squad, plus they were on his side of town and they were still tripping on him. Babygurl couldn't lie and say the nigga wasn't fine and fly as hell, because he was. He was tall with caramel skin, with a drop fade and a smile the ladies couldn't resist. His fit was all black, which made him look more gangsta than his pretty boy looks. Without even acknowledging the rest of the crew, she walked to the back of the truck with her girls right behind her and was surprised at what she was looking at. The truck was full from wall to wall and floor to roof with bricks. The only room that was left was for the four niggas that had jumped out.

"Y'all on a whole different level now," said Twan.

"We been on a whole different level. We about to put you on the money train and shit is real right now, so them li'l hittas you got betta be trained to go." She turned around to walk off, but stopped. "Oh yeah. I run this shit, and don't ever forget. Now unload this shit, because I got shit to do."

As she walked off, Sadie and Ladie started laughing because he was looking stupid as hell. He shook his head as he and his goons started unloading the truck. While they unloaded the truck, Babygurl was making phone calls to every trap to let them know that everything was all good and their spot would be loaded up by the end of the day. She wasn't tripping about Quick robbing her for the last of her work, but she was pissed off about him thinking shit was sweet on her end.

It took them a couple of hours to unload and pack up the bricks they had to distribute to the trap houses. They had 200 bricks of powder and were still waiting on the heroin to be delivered. She couldn't wait for Kilo to get out because she knew he would make the right moves with a connect like this. So while he and the rest of the squad were waiting to come home, she and her girls were gon' take over everything they could.

She was snapped out of her thoughts when Sean's cousin came busting through the door. All at once, everybody who was in the apartment had guns pointed to his head.

"Hold up!" Baby Jay yelled.

"Nigga, don't be runnin up in this bitch like that knowin' the streets real right now," Sean said as everybody put their guns away.

He sat down and explained everything that went down with Quick and Savage. Babygurl sat back and listened to his story, and all she could do as laugh. Everybody looked at her like she was crazy except Kiesha, who had her eyes on Sean. It amazed her how he could be so calm in all this shit. Something about him was off, and she was gon' bring it up to Babygurl ASAP.

"Let that nigga have that shit. We on a whole 'notha level now. Right now, we load up the traps and make sure every soldier we got straight, because we about to take over, so y'all betta be ready to bust ya guns," Babygurl said, then walked out.

With a new connect and a team of ridas, she was ready to tear the streets up. It was time for her grimy ways to come out, because she needed the streets to remember just what the squad was about.

***

Lexi was riding shotgun to Quick while Savage and Lovey rode in the backseat. They had the car full of kush smoke while Money-bagg Yo was busting through the speakers. Lexi had to convince Lovey to ride with Savage so she could start putting her plan together. She hated that she couldn't tell her sister what was going on, but right now her sister was basically riding with the other team. The only thing that was on her mind was getting back right with her baby daddy, no matter what it took. Today was the first time Quick was taking her to one of his stash spots, and while she was excited, she had to play it cool. She hit the blunt, then passed it back to Quick. She needed to do everything possible to stay on his good side, so she leaned over and whispered in his ear.

"Tell her she can't have none if I ain't involved," she said with a smirk on her face.

What she said caught him off guard because his eyes got big. He didn't know she was watching his text the whole time.

"Be careful what you ask for," he shot back.

"I'm game. Just set it up." She reached over and squeezed his dick. Kilo had already put her on game about Valerie just like he hipped Valerie about her. She had planned on using her to get closer to him, so she played her part to the T. Before she knew it, they were pulling up to an apartment complex off Pinn Road. She could tell there was a bunch of money out this way because it looked like a mini–Las Vegas strip. The apartments was jumping even though it was 1:00 in the morning.

They stepped out and all the attention was immediately turned to them. Hustlas and dopefiends ran up to Quick and Savage like they were rap stars. Quick was eating good out of nowhere and she didn't like the fact that Kilo was locked up while he was out here living lavish. She could tell that Lovey had the same thoughts because Correy was still locked up.

They made their way to the very back of the apartments where niggas was posted up with straps in their hands ready for anything to jump off. When she stepped inside, it looked like Quick had two apartments gutted and turned into one. There was so much money being counted up that her mouth dropped to the floor. For all the money, there was ten times the amount of coke, heroin, weed, and guns. She took in everything as she and Lovey sat on the loveseat closest to the door. She watched as a nigga came up to Quick and whispered something in his ear. He looked at Savage, gave him a head nod, then Savage and two other niggas left.

"My, bad li'l mama, but I gotta handle this li'l problem real quick, then I got a proposition for you."

She and Lovey looked at each other with confusion because that last statement caught them off guard. Whatever his proposition was, she didn't want no parts of it. She just wanted Kilo's loyalty, and that's it. She heard commotion coming through the door as two niggas were being dragged in by Savage and the niggas that had left with him.

"So, these are the niggas that been bitin' the hand that feeds them," said Quick.

"These li'l niggas almost got away with they scary asses. I should've shot they asses just for making me run. You know what?" He said fuck it, took out his burner, and shot one in the foot and the other one in the knee. "Try to run now, bitch-ass nigga."

She and Lovey sat there keeping their cool because that gangsta shit wasn't nothing new to them since their niggas were Kilo and Correy. Quick walked up to the niggas, lit a blunt, and just smirked.

"My li'l homies tell me y'all two li'l niggas tried to run off with a li'l bit over $300,000. Now that is a nice li'l piece of change, huh?" he asked Savage.

"A li'l bit too much," he responded.

"So what made y'all wanna do some dumb-ass shit like that, knowin' y'all wasn't gon' get away?" he asked them.

He waited for a few seconds, and when no answer came out, he gave a slight chuckle because he admired their gangsta. Before anyone in the apartment knew it, he was on the closest one to him, pistol whipping him like he wanted to get at Babygurl. He eased up off of the nigga before he could lose consciousness.

"For any one of you niggas thinking that you can run off with some of my money, let these niggas be an example."

He upped his other 9mm and began to empty both his clips into their faces. Everybody in the apartment was quiet as the shots clapped into their skulls. Lexi sat unfazed but hated the nigga more and more with every shot. He looked at her when he was done and she saw pure evil. She smiled. If only he knew that Kilo's mind was plotting on him at this moment, he wouldn't have that much confidence.

"Y'all clean this shit up. I got business to talk."

He walked to the back as Lexi and Lovey got up to follow them along with Savage. They went to a room that looked like a mini office. They all sat down on the furniture and poured up shots of Hennessey.

"So, what's this business deal?"

"We want y'all to make a move that only females could do."

"And what's that?"

"Drop off to some white dude for us."

"Hell naw, nigga, is you stupid? Correy would trip on yo' ass for suggesting some shit like that!" Lovey yelled his way, but before he could say something back, Lexi jumped in.

"Yeah, we'll do it, but half of it comes to us," she said with a serious tone.

He smiled and nodded his head because he wasn't tripping on the pay and was respecting the hustle. She only agreed to do it so she could let Babygurl know about as much as she could, plus she needed to stack some bread for her and her sister because in the end, she knew this would all end up in a big war.

Chapter 12

Kilo was walking down the corridor of the Bexar County Jail quickly because he had gotten an attorney visit out of nowhere. He was happy to be seeing Bianca, but he hoped she had some kind of good news. He looked up and down the hall, waiting for niggas to try him out.

When he walked into the visiting booth, Bianca was already there waiting for him. She looked good in the black business dress she was wearing, even though it was tight around her stomach.

"Hey beautiful. How you and the baby doing?" he asked, then looked down at her belly.

"We good. I got your daughter, so she good too."

"Good. Now tell me you got some good news for a nigga."

"Well, tell your boys that the girls put up the money for the same judge you got to take their cases. And you will be home in a month. Nobody knows about it yet because I want you to pop up on the scene and shake it up."

"Hell yeah, that's what the fuck I'm talkin' about!"

Even though he had been locked up, he always knew what was going on because she kept her ear to the street for him. Babygurl had been holding down the streets and had made some major moves, and now that he was coming home, he now was even more anxious to smoke Correy so he could take over San Antonio. This was the second time she had come through for him, so he knew he had to show her his appreciation some kind of way.

They chopped it up for a little bit more about what he needed her and Valerie to do before the visit was over. He walked back to his tank like nothing had changed because he didn't want to risk anybody putting the word out that he was going home.

***

"I'm telling you, you should have gone ahead and let me smoke that bitch and get it out of the way," Savage said as he passed the blunt to Quick. They sat in one of Quick's trap houses on the northeast side with four of his shooters just in case Babygurl and the bitches came through tripping. He was far from scared of Babygurl, but he did respect her gangsta. He felt where Savage was coming from, but he had to be patient and wait on Kilo so they could end of all this shit at one time.

"Man, fuck that bitch. She the least of my worries. Right now, I'm tryna stack these blue faces and get rich," Quick said as he got ready to serve the dopefiend that was at the back door. Through the streets he knew that Babygurl had found a new plug because besides his dope, it was some fire flooding every hood that he didn't run. He had Pablo trying to figure out who was hitting her with that good shit, but he kept coming up empty-handed. It was pissing him off more and more that a bitch kept out-thinking him. He and Savage continued to make the money that came through until Jessica and her cousin came through to help count it so they could get it to Pablo. Pablo would get this payment and the next early so he could focus on taking over more spots.

While he and Savage floated on a Sweet back and forth, he heard somebody's system beating down the block. Quick looked out of one of the front windows and noticed a navy-blue Cadillac XTS pulling up. His first instinct was to pull out his banga, and everybody in the trap did the same thing. The squad had his ass on point. But when Jessica and Laura jumped out, all he did was smile and put his strap up. He watched as they walked up the sidewalk in those little bitty-ass shorts that showed off their smooth legs and fat-ass pussy. He couldn't wait to max her li'l ass out because he was feeling her, and he knew with her on his team, he was on his way to the top.

He opened the door and Jessica jumped him with her legs and arms wrapped around him. As she kissed him, his dick started rising, so he sat her down.

"I missed you, papi," she said as she licked her lips.

"I missed you too, li'l mama. But let's handle this business first," he said as he and Jessica walked to the back room. He saw Savage and Jessica do the same as his li'l homies got on point and took their positions.

Once he closed the door, he went straight to the closet and pulled out three duffle bags, then tossed them on the bed where Jessica was sitting. He was glad to be getting this money to Pablo, because them bitches were out to take whatever they could at any time.

It took them a few hours and a few blunts to count everything that was in the duffle bags. Quick smiled as they stacked the money back into the duffle bags because there was more where that came from. At the sight of Quick and all that money, Jessica's pussy instantly got wet. Of course she was used to being around money due to her family, but she never had a boss nigga like Quick.

Quick looked up and noticed the way she was looking at him, which made his dick hard on sight. She came out of her tank top, then removed her bra and revealed the most perfect titties he'd ever seen. She pulled down her shorts and thong at the same time and once Quick saw that pretty pussy, he attacked her li'l ass. He laid her down on the edge of the bed as he went straight to her titties. He sucked on her nipples like he was making love. He kissed down her stomach because he couldn't wait to taste that pussy. He was gon' take his time, but once he saw the way she was leaking, he dove in headfirst.

"Oh shit! Papi! Please!" she begged as she cuffed the back of his head with both of her hands.

Quick made sure he smacked on every part of her pussy, then sucked and licked on her clit.

"I'm about to cum!"

Once she yelled that, he stabbed the inside with his tongue. She tried to get away, but Quick locked her legs. He continued to eat her pussy just to make sure she knew he was boss. He let her go, then stood up and took his clothes off. Once she saw his dick escape his boxers, her eyes damn near popped out of her head.

"Don't get scared now." He stepped in front of her so she could handle her business.

She reached for his dick and jacked it off and sucked on the head at the same time. She knew she was gon' have trouble sucking his dick, but she sure was gon' try.

"Damn, papi, you got a lot of dick. Shit!"

She spit on his dick and stuffed as much as she could in her mouth. When she looked up and saw his head tilted back, she went into overdrive while slobbering, jacking and gagging on only half of his dick. Her jaws had started to hurt because he was too thick, so she stood up and bent over the bed, then looked back at him. Her ass was plump, but her li'l slim ass had a fat pussy, and he planned on punishing every part of it. He rubbed his dick head up and down her slit, then slowly pushed in. As soon as he put the tip in, she started running, but he grabbed her waist and long-stroked that pussy.

"Oh fuck! Baby, it's too…much! I'm coming!!" she yelled as she stuffed her face into the bed.

Quick knew she was coming ASAP because his dick was white already.

"Damn, li'l mama, this pussy good. Whose pussy is this!" he said while smacking her ass.

"Yours, daddy. Yours!"

He was only halfway in and he was already hitting the bottom. He flipped her over, then threw both of her legs over his shoulders. He slid back inside of her with ease, but she was still tight as hell.

"Fuck!" she yelled. "Fuck me with this big-ass dick, papi! Please!"

When she said that, he started pounding her shit with everything he had. She was hemmed up, so she had to take every inch he was giving her. She was regretting saying what she said because he was in her stomach. It felt like her insides were on fire as he fucked the shit out of her. Even though she was in pain, it felt good to finally get some black dick.

"I'm finna come!" he groaned.

"Give it to me! Cum in this pussy. It's yours, papi," she said as she met him thrust for thrust. She knew he was cumming because it felt like he was growing more in her stomach.

Once he was done, he laid next to her while she laid her head on his chest.

"Baby, you got a whole lot of dick," was the first thing she said.

All he could do was laugh. He knew what he was packing, and most bitches couldn't handle it, but she stood under that pressure like a champ. He was feeling Jessica, so he needed to find a way to tell her father. This beef with Babygurl was getting real, so he couldn't afford to lose his plug.

"Quick, before we drop that money off to my father, I want to show you this spot that will help you out."

"Oh yeah? How is it gon' help me out?"

"First off, my cousin's got an army of killas on his side. And second, the hood I'm tryna show you makes no less than $20,000 a day. I told you to stick with me, and I got you."

"Alright, let's make that move right now," he said, then got up to get dressed.

Once they got everything together, he and Savage jumped in the same whip, then followed Jessica and Laura to the Southside with all four of his shooters behind them. No matter what, wherever he was going or who he was with, he always made sure he kept some killas with him. After that little stunt those twins did, he didn't trust nobody.

He turned up the Moneybagg Yo that was playing, lit up a Newport, and thought about everything that had led up to this point.

Ray Vinci

Chapter 13

Babygurl had just gotten the call from Bianca a couple of hours ago about one of Quick's spots off of Pinn Road. She knew it was because of Lexi that Bianca was hitting her with this info, but it was still hard for her to like her because of how she'd played Kilo. If it was up to her, she would've been put her next to her baby sister Lisa.

Her, Sean, his brother, and two cousins were on the way to Skinnie's block to meet up with her girls so they could go take Quick's spot. She and Sean had been up all night trapping and counting money, so she was already on edge. Bianca had also told her that Agent Long would make sure that the coast was clear and that none of his people would be around the area for at least an hour.

She really didn't know too much about Pinn Road, but she did know that there was a bunch of money over that way.

"So, what's the plan?" Sean asked from the driver's seat.

"Shit, smoke everything that ain't with us. I want everything this nigga got: dope, money, and respect," she said as Sean pulled into Culebra Meat Market off of Ferris Avenue. The block was jumping, but her focus was on her girls.

Sean parked next to Kiesha's all black Kia as his brother and cousins pulled in next to them.

When she stepped out, everybody on the block showed her some love and asked about Kilo. Due to this being Kilo's hood, niggas mugged Sean and all his people, hoping that they did something stupid. She hugged her girls, then gave them the rundown on everything that Bianca had told her. Once everything was settled, they were on their way to Pinn Road four cars deep. Babygurl put in Li'l' Boosie's "Mind of a Maniac" and listened to it over and over the whole way to get in killa mode. It took them twenty minutes to get to Pinn Road and Babygurl was already loving what she was seeing.

Pinn Road was a long-ass street that looked like a Las Vegas strip. Dopefiends and prostitutes stood on every corner. She told Sean to drive up and down the strip so they could check the spots out, plus she needed to find the exact apartments Quick was hustling out of. Once she spotted where all of the traffic was going, they followed them. All four cars headed towards the back. She noticed that there was an exit in the back and smiled because this was too easy. Her and Sean checked their straps, then stepped out as her squad did the same.

"Y'all already know what's up now that we here," she said mainly to her girls, because they had been there before. "We gon' walk through this bitch, push up, and step on some toes, and fa' sho' one of the people that's running this bitch gon' come out." Babygurl was confident in her girls, so she knew it would be easy to stomp down.

As they walked through, everybody had eyes on them due to them not being from out there, plus they were some bad bitches, and Sean and his boys made their presence known. Once they got to the basketball court, they then knew this was the hot spot of the hood.

"Oh yeah, I can see right now I'm gon' like it out here!" Baby Jay said once he got to looking at all of the hoes that came through.

All of them laughed because they were thinking the same thing.

Babygurl and her girls watched as Sean, Baby Jay, and his two cousins bossed up and started running shit, and even though he wasn't Kilo, he was still stomp down, and that shit made Babygurl like him even more. They sat down at the nearest park tables, then instantly set up shop.

To Babygurl's surprise, the money started rolling in no time. All she did was laugh to herself because muthafuckas knew what money looked like. It took longer than they thought for the niggas that were running shit to come out and see why the money stopped flowing their way.

"Now y'all know y'all can't come up in here stepping on toes like that," the short light-skinned one said with his hands behind his back. He was flanked by two tall Mexicans that were tatted up everywhere.

"Shit, we just tryna find us a new spot to hustle out of, and this bitch jumping like a house party," Sean said as he counted the stack of twenties he'd just made.

The rest of the squad was ready to trip because the two Mexicans had their straps at their side.

"Well, this spot is occupied, but if you tryna get down, I can call my big homie Quick——"

He never got to finish his sentence because once Babygurl heard Quick's name she put a hole the size of a quarter in his forehead. Before the two Mexicans could react, Kiesha and Cassy riddled their bodies with bullets. Their bodies didn't even get the chance to hit the ground before choppa bullets were flying their way. They all ducked under the tables and behind trees and looked to see where the shots were coming from. Baby Jay was the first one to spot two niggas hanging out windows on the top floor. They stayed put until they ran out of bullets, and then Babygurl and her squad took off towards where the three niggas had come from while Sean and his fam took off for the niggas with the choppas.

As soon as they rounded the corner, bullets were being sprayed their way. Sadie was the first to let her gun clap as she dropped two of them with ease. Ladie was right behind her twin, hitting anything that wasn't with them. Most of the people had already run inside, when the first shot rang out, so it was just them and the ops. Babygurl was at the door that was already open, and she immediately let loose on the group of niggas that were still counting money at the table.

She heard movement in the back, so her and Kiesha quickly moved that way. She opened the first door and saw two little boys that looked no older than 14 and 15. Kiesha upped her burner and was about to smoke 'em when Babygurl stopped her.

"Hold up! Why you two li'l niggas in this bitch?" Babygurl asked.

"Savage is our cousin. We was just tryna make some money so we could help our momma out," the older one said.

She looked at them. They reminded her of Kilo and Illy. "Well, today is y'all lucky day. Tell Quick and Savage that they're next, and the next time he steps foot in my spot, he dead." She then turned around and left.

Her and her girls met up with Sean and his boys where they split up.

"Baby Jay, you and Sadie can have this spot," she said as they made their way to their whips, then headed back to the other side of town.

***

Quick and Savage were making their rounds to every trap, picking up the re-up money so they could re-cop. They had just pulled out of the Wheatly Courts when Savage's phone rang. He was gon' let it ring until he saw his little cousin's number pop op on the screen. He turned the music down and Quick looked at him like he was crazy.

"What's up, cuz? Talk to me," he said through the phone. As he listened to his kinfolk explain to him about what had gone down, Quick watched his face turn red as hell.

"Alright, we on our way right now!" Savage yelled in the phone, then hung up. "FUCK! FUCK! FUCK! This bitch done hit us up again!"

"How the fuck did this bitch know about that spot!" he said through clenched as he made a U-turn on Walters Street. He was mad as hell as he sped towards I-35. He was so mad that he never saw the white van four cars behind him. What he did see was the police lights coming from the unmarked car that was right behind him.

"Fuck! Tuck the burners and be calm.," Quick said as he pulled over. He couldn't afford to run because he knew that if he did, he would get caught and spend some time in jail, plus he had over $100,000, on him so he had to be smart.

They both tucked their guns under their seats, then straightened up. Quick looked out the side mirror and saw that it was Detective Stronbone and knew what time it was. When Detective Stronbone made it to the car, he tapped on the window. For some reason, that shit pissed Quick off, but he still rolled down the window.

"How may I help you, sir?" Quick asked with a fake smile.

"Well, well, well, if it isn't Mr. I-don't-wanna-be-found. I been looking all over San Antonio for your black ass. Tell me how come out of you, Correy, Kilo, and his boys, you the only one I couldn't get?"

"Sir, I don't know what you're talking about. I'm a law-abiding citizen," Quick said, sounding proper.

This made Savage stifle a laugh, which made Detective Stronbone hot.

"I can take both y'all black asses to jail right now, because I know y'all got enough money in here to go fed. But see, here's the thing. I know Babygurl wants your head, so I'ma try my luck that way, plus you and her got a nightmare coming y'all's way." He walked away laughing out loud.

They both sat back and let out deep breaths. Quick sat there until he saw Detective Stronbone turn the corner. He grabbed his heat, set it on his lap, looked at Savage, then they both busted out laughing. He pulled off slow, then turned on East Carson so he could get on I-35 and see what was up with his spot.

Pinn Road was his number one spot and not too many people knew about it. Before he could even think about who it could be, he saw a white van pull on the side of him. The side door slid open and two Asian-looking muthafuckas hung out with Uzis aimed their way. Bullets riddled the side of the car but didn't do much damage because Quick sped up. The van was right behind them as the passenger hung out of the window sending shot after shot their way.

"Nigga, you betta get us the fuck away from this van or put us in a position so we can bust back!" Savage yelled over the gunfire.

"Who the fuck is them niggas!" Quick yelled as he busted a left off of East Carson. He hit the brakes so the van could get in front and Savage could get some shots off, but he instantly regretted that move because the rear doors busted open and two more Asians let loose on the car.

Quick and Savage ducked down as he put the car in reverse, then backed up blindly. He had to think of a plan and quick, because they hadn't even been able to get off one shot.

As soon as he thought it, the bullets stopped, and Savage wasted no time as he finger-fucked his trigger praying that they at least hit one of them punk-ass Asians. They were not too far from Savage's spot, so Quick hit the block and made his way to Muncey Street. Savage was still dumping on the van as he hung out of his window. He saw the front glass shatter as the driver swerved off onto another street.

"Nigga, get us to the spot ASAP so we can figure out what the fuck is going on!" said Savage as he sat back in his seat.

Quick pressed the gas as a million thoughts ran through his mind.

Chapter 14

Detective Stronbone was loving the way things were going his way. He wanted Babygurl and her squad bad, plus Quick was building an empire of his own, so he had to play his cards right. If he could get one of the squads to take the other one out, it would make his job a lot easier. But just in case that didn't work, he had a backup plan he had to put in motion before it blew up in his face. Right now, he was on his way to meet up with that important piece for an update. Even though he had enough to put them all away, he felt like it was bigger than it seemed.

The ride from the Eastside to the North was slow due to traffic. He rode in silence due to him trying to think, so he heard his phone vibrate on the passenger seat. He looked over and saw that it was the Chief of Police and automatically knew something was up. He reached over, answered it, then put in on speakerphone.

"Talk to me, Chief," he said as he drove.

"You tell me what the hell is going on. There was a deadly shootout on Pinn Road that left bodies everywhere and nobody wants to talk. Then, not even thirty minutes later, I get a call saying that it sounded like a war was going on up and down East Carson Street. Get to them ASAP and find out what the hell is going on in my city!"

He hung up before Detective Stronbone even got a chance to respond back. He was pissed off because he knew that Quick had something to do with the shootout on East Carson since he had just left from there. He was going to turn back around, but he was closer to Pinn Road. It took him five minutes to get there, and even though he didn't know the location he knew that his fellow officers would be out there. He drove all the way down until he spotted all of the action. He found a spot to park, then stepped out.

He flashed his ID and badge to the officer, then stepped under the crime scene tape. He walked around, making sure not to step on any evidence. There were bodies inside and outside with triple amount of bullets, and he instantly knew that this had Babygurl's name written all over it. He knew from the past that her people were ruthless, and he couldn't wait to take them down. Too many bodies were dropping because of this war that had been going on, and he couldn't wait until they were either locked up or dead.

It took him a few hours to wrap things up, then he headed back to the other side of town, hoping things weren't too bad. He was exhausted and pissed off because he had missed his meeting with the one person that could at least help him a little bit. He hit the freeway, texted his little helper a later date to meet, then prepared himself for whatever waited for him on the east side.

***

Lexi had just dropped Lovey off at her apartment so she could get up with Valerie. She and Lovey had just finished making their second drop for Quick and Savage, and even though Lovey hated it, she loved the money they were making. Lexi hated to hide what she was up to, but she had to. She had been visiting Kilo at least once a week so she could lace him up on what Quick had going on and so that he could lace her up as well, which was also why she was getting up with Valerie.

She had never been to the northwest side, and she instantly felt the change in the atmosphere as she existed off Highway 90 and Babcock Road. When she made it to the address that Valerie had texted her, she was in awe since she was from the eastside, and most of the houses out that way were either falling apart or abandoned. She text Valerie to let her know that she was parked outside, then waited for her to come out. Lexy didn't know what to expect of Valerie. All she knew was that she was a lawyer and would help Correy out and that she was Bianca's cousin. She had found herself liking Bianca more and more and she hoped Valerie was like her.

When Valerie stepped out of the front door Lexi couldn't help but notice how bad she was. From the way she was dressed, Lexi would've never known she was a lawyer. She had her long black hair tied in a ponytail, which made her blue eyes stand out. Her neck, ears, fingers, and wrists were dressed in jewelry that could only come from Tiffany's. Her black Dior jeans hugged her hips like they were painted on her, and her black and white Dior halter top dipped low enough to give a good view of her breasts. She had on some black and white Retro 11's, which made Lexi nod her head in approval. She slid in the passenger seat and her Fendi perfume instantly filled the car.

"Hi, I'm Valerie," she said to Lexi, which made her realize she was staring.

"I'm Lexi," she said as she pulled off.

"So where to, since Kilo got everybody on these crazy ass missions?" she said as she dug in her purse. "Do you mind if I smoke this blunt in here?"

"No just make sure you pass it. And since when did lawyers smoke?"

"Since me."

They both laughed, and Lexi knew she was gon' like Valerie. They hit the blunt as Chris Brown played in the background and Lexi kept sneaking glances at her. Valerie turned the music down and looked at Lexi.

"You keep looking at me like you don't trust me. Speak your mind."

Lexi hesitated before she spoke. "I'm not gon' lie. I trust whateva Kilo has going on, so it's not that. I can't help but stare because you and your cousin are some bad-ass white bitches."

"Thank you, and you look good yourself."

"Alright, first things first. Kilo wants you to get in good with that detective that's on his case. You and Bianca are the only ones out of us all that he don't know. I'm pretty sure he's got a nice payout for you at the end of it all. Second, I want to see what's up with Quick's new bitch. Babygurl got something planned, so we need to follow her and see what she got going on," Lexi explained as she parked down the street not even ten minutes away from where she picked up Valerie.

"Okay. So why are we stopping here, if you don't mind me asking?"

"Your kinfolk gave Babygurl this address for her to give to you. Detective Stronbone and his wife live here, so now you have a starting point. You shouldn't have a problem with getting up with him," Lexi said, looking her up and down.

"Cool. Well, you tell Kilo that I got Correy a release date, plus me and Bianca will be working on his boys' case, which they should be getting out pretty soon too."

"Okay. Now let's go see what's up with Quick's bitch."

She drove off with a smile on her face because things were looking good for her so far.

Chapter 15

Babygurl had told everybody to meet her at the count house in Gold-field Apartments. Sean, Baby Jay, Li'l Tony, and Rob sat at the table counting money. Twan and his Asian hittas were on alert with the Dracos at every window. Babygurl, Kiesha, Cassy, Sadie, and Ladie were sitting in the living room also counting money. She had to make sure every dollar was there because Tree was blessing their game. They would re-up at least once every two weeks, and at the rate that shit was going, her whole team would be hood rich. She lit a blunt, then handed it to Sean, who was lost in the money count.

She looked around the room and was happy at the way things had turned out. Kilo, Illy, Felony, and Slugga would be with them soon, and she couldn't wait. She stood up, went to the back room, then came back with a mini Gucci duffle bag.

"Look out, everybody!" she said, getting everybody's attention. "Me and my girls wanna give y'all something to show our appreciation to y'all."

She dug in the bag and pulled out nine squad up chains that were busted down with black diamonds. It was just like the chains that Kilo had given them when the money had started getting good for the squad. It was just like the chains she, Kiesha, Cassy, Sadie, and Ladie had on. She handed each one of her girls one, then gave the other four to Twan's hittas. She put one around Sean's neck as she watched her girls do the same to the rest. Sadie walked up to Baby Jay and straddled his lap as she put the chain on. He gripped her fat ass as she dipped her head to kiss him. His dick instantly got rock hard. She could do nothing else but grind on it, because he had a good grip on her ass cheeks.

"Damn, boy, you got all this dick," she said in his ear. "You gon' handle up or what?"

"I got you, shawty."

She stood up, then turned to walk back to her girls. He smacked her ass and watched it jiggle in the cut-off shorts that were hugging her ass cheeks. He had her pussy wet as fuck just with that little encounter and she couldn't wait to see what that dick was talking about. Babygurl was about to say something until she was stopped by her phone. She looked at it and couldn't help but smile at what she was reading.

"Alright, y'all, I got to handle some business real quick, but tonight we gon' shut down Bar 11." She went to the back room and closed the door. She went to her safe that was tucked in the corner of her closet. She dropped the mini Gucci duffle bag in front of it, then entered the code. When it opened, she instantly grabbed stacks of hundreds and loaded the bag up. She zipped up the bag, locked the safe back up, and was headed out of the door. Before she could get out, Kiesha came in and closed the door.

"Bitch, what you got going on?" she asked her best friend.

"Bianca just texted me and told me to meet her in Canyon Lake so we could go half on a house," Babygurl said, trying to keep it short as possible.

"And?" Kiesha added because she knew that there was more to it. She hadn't seen Babygurl smile that hard since before Kilo got locked up.

"She said that Kilo is coming home, but he can't be seen in San Antonio city limits, so we copping a house for him in Canyon Lake. Slugga, Illy, and Felony gon' be right behind him."

Kiesha had a big-ass smile on her face and wanted to scream in excitement, but she knew the important of keeping it a secret.

"So that means Correy getting out too."

Babygurl nodded her head in agreement and they both knew what time it was one everybody was out. Shit was about to get real in a few weeks, so she wanted to make sure they were ready to ride. Without saying anything else, they walked back up front. As they stepped outside of the room, Li'l Tony was reading a text, but quickly stuffed his phone in his pocket, which made Babygurl look at him suspiciously. She kept it moving as she put the little incident on the back of her mind.

She told her squad she would meet up with them at Bar 11 around 10:00 p.m., then left out the front door with the duffle bag over her shoulder. She jumped in her AMG, then peeled out of Goldfield. It took her no time to get there due to her speeding. She rode through the neighborhood and liked what she saw. This was a good duck-off spot for Kilo to chill until it was time to get the squad back together. She was gon' text Bianca to see where she was until she spotted the black BMW and her standing outside of it with a black man in a dress suit, whom she assumed was a realtor.

Babygurl parked behind Bianca, then stepped out looking like new money. She hugged Bianca, then shook hands with the realtor.

"So, what's good?" she asked Bianca.

"This bad boy is going to run us $500,000 and it's gon' be in Kilo's name," said Bianca.

"Shit, I got $250,000 in the backseat right now."

"Cool. Let's fill out the paperwork so we can get things settled," said the agent.

He walked towards the house with them right behind. Babygurl couldn't wait for her ride or die to come home, so they could push Quick's and Correy's ass off the streets. She had a newfound respect for Bianca and was happy for Kilo to have somebody like her.

**

It had been a minute since Tree had been to a club, so when Babygurl and his twins had asked him to go out with him, he took them up on their offer. He was gon' dress down but decided to keep it plain. He had on some smoke grey Polo jeans that fitted him just right, a black purple label button down shirt, and some black and grey Polo loafers. The necklace, earrings, watch, and bracelet that he had just gotten imported from Japan were busting at every angle. Even though he was dressed like a regular dopeboy, he was gon' ride like a boss. When he stepped out, his black-on-black Maybach was just pulling up to the front with Twan's four hittas in a black F-250. He slid in the back and Twan handed him a glass of Hennessey.

"What's up, nephew?" he said, then dapped him up as the driver drove off.

"Shit, this money."

"I see Babygurl got ya pockets right."

"Hell yeah! Li'l mama 'bout her paper, and she a gangsta," Twan said, then hit his cup. He had been hearing about Kilo and his squad from the jump, so he knew what they were all about. When Kilo and his boys got locked up, he thought that it was the end of the infamous squad until Sadie and Ladie came to him for help. He was glad he looked out for Babygurl and her squad, because the money was coming in like never before. Tree had been doing a little digging on this nigga Quick and found out he was plugged in with the Mexican Mafia. He was snapped out of his thoughts when Twan had told him they were at the club.

They waited for Twan's shooter to park the truck, then they stepped out. Tree walked up to the bouncer, whispered something in his ear, handed him a roll of money, then looked back. The bouncer nodded his head, stuffed the roll in his pocket, then stepped to the side. Twan was loving the status that his uncle had because he wasn't feeling going in the club without his gun. When they stepped in, Drake was bumping through the speakers as hoes and niggas were dancing all over each other.

He looked up and saw that Babygurl had the two corner VIP sections occupied. The girls had one and the niggas had the other one on lock. He noticed that Babygurl had two bad-ass white girls with her. He had to admit that Babygurl and her girls were killing shit. They had to be the baddest bitches in the club. He was gon' sit with the niggas, but Babygurl waved him over. He stepped in and two of Twan's shooters stood outside and guarded the booth. He hugged his twins, then sat next to Babygurl as she handed him a bottle of 1800.

"I'm glad you could make it," she said as she sat back.

"Me too. It's been a while since I been out. I see y'all got this bitch on smash. I need to come out more often," he said as he poured himself a cup of 1800.

"Well, enjoy yourself. Everything on me. As a matter of fact…" She reached in her Fendi bag and pulled out two stacks of hundreds, then handed them to Kiesha. "Buy the bar out, then tell the DJ we in this bitch."

"Oh! I'm liking the way you roll," Tree said as Kiesha left. He couldn't help but look at her ass. It took all of ten minutes for her to come back, and as soon as she stepped back in the booth, the DJ cut the music down.

"Awww shit! We got the squad in this bitch, and they just bought the bar out, so drinks on them. And shout out to the big homie Tree of the Money Train Mafia. Turn up!" he said, then Young Thug was busting through the club as the whole club raised their bottles and cups up. Both VIP booths stood up and acknowledged the club with bottles of their own.

Tree watched as hoes walked up to the VIP booth but was shut down because the girls started flexing and ran 'em off. He watched as the girls started shaking their asses and niggas instantly tried to holla until Sean and his team started tripping.

All Tree could do was laugh because they reminded him of when his team had finally made it to the top. He was having fun and felt like nothing could fuck up his night until he looked up and saw a longtime enemy of his. He instantly mugged up and Babygurl saw it, then followed his gaze to the VIP that was on the balcony.

"You know that nigga?" she asked, ready to trip.

"Yeah, that's Pablo. He's the head nigga over the Mexican Mafia and he is Quick's new connect," he said as he continued to mug Pablo.

Once she heard Mexican Mafia and Quick's new connect, she began to put two and two together. She was wondering how Quick was plugged in without Correy. He came up too fast, and now she knew why.

"So what's up. You tryna step to him or what?"

"Naw, right now ain't the time."

The whole squad must've seen how Tree and Babygurl was masked up and were ready for whatever. Tree knew that Pablo didn't like how Babygurl flexed on all the ballers in the club by buying the bar out, plus it didn't make it better that he was in the club. Even though Tree told her now was not the time, she still wanted to let the nigga know that shit wasn't Sweet on her end, but

Bianca and Valerie was with them and she didn't want to hear Kilo's mouth about her being out and pregnant.

She saw him get on his phone real quick, then hang up. She already knew that he was calling Quick, so she had to get Bianca and Valerie out before shit got too real. She put her squad on game, so when she stood to leave, both VIPs did the same. As she exited the club, she was already making plans to get at Pablo.

Chapter 16

Quick rode down W.W. White on his way to his trap in Skyline. He had let this spot go due to it not producing enough money, but as of lately, it had been jumping, plus Correy was coming home, so he needed as many spots as possible. He was happy his homie was coming home. He was already planning to throw his nigga the biggest block party the city had ever seen.

Savage was in the passenger seat with twin Glock 9's in his lap, chain-smoking Newports back-to-back. Ever since the Asians had hit them up a week ago they were ready to let anybody have it.

Quick had put word out that if anybody knew who the Asians were, they would receive a nice sum of money. They both kept looking in their rearview mirrors to make sure their li'l homies were behind them. They had got caught slipping once, but Quick would be damned if he let it happen again. His phone had vibrated on the center console, indicating that he had just received a text. He saw that it was the lawyer that had gotten Correy out and he opened it.

She gave him the address to a motel so they could meet up so he could pay her the $20,000 that she had charged him. Without texting her back, he set his phone back down. As soon as he set it down, it rang. He knew it was Pablo because of the ringtone. Savage turned the music down as he picked it up.

"Talk to me, big homie," he said through the phone.

"Que pasa, Quick? How are thing going for you?"

"It's good, but I know you didn't call me just to see how I was doing. What's on ya mind?"

Pablo laughed. He was liking Quick more and more with every conversation that they had. He was sharp and reminded him of a certain person that he had really forgotten about until last night.

"You, my friend, but what I need to discuss with you can't be talked about over the phone," Pablo said.

"Say no more, big homie. Give me the time and place, and I'm there."

"In two hours, meet me at my family restaurant. I will text you the address. Take care, Quick, and I'll see you in a bit," Pablo said then hung up.

Now Quick was anxious to know what he wanted to speak with him about. He was about to turn into Skyline when he spotted a car that he knew all too well. Instead of turning, he stayed straight and got right behind the car. He knew Kiesha's car from anywhere.

"Nigga, you missed the turn," Savage said, looking at him crazy.

"I think that's that bitch Kiesha." Quick was focused on the car, which made Savage do the same thing. He didn't know them bitches like Quick did, but he didn't give a fuck because them hoes were doing too much.

"Pull up on the side of that bitch so I can light her ass up."

"Let's see where she go. She might be goin' to where them other bitches at."

He followed her all the way to Dietrich Road. She pressed in the code, then waited for the gate to open. He wanted to let loose on her shit so bad but had to be patient. She drove inside the gate with him right behind her and his li'l homies right behind them. He followed her all the way to the back as his adrenaline rushed. She parked in front of an apartment, and he instantly remembered this spot. He and his goons parked across the street and waited for her to get out.

He saw her get on the phone and he knew that she was calling Babygurl to come out. He saw a door in the breezeway open and at the same time, Kiesha stepped out with bags of food in her hand. Just as she made it to the other side of the car, Quick and Savage stepped out busting their straps. Kiesha was hit in the leg, shoulder, and back and instantly dropped as Babygurl, Cassy, Sadie, and Ladie let loose from the breezeway, making them duck for cover.

When Quick's li'l homies saw them duck for cover, they jumped out of their truck with choppas and lit up everything that was in front of them. All four of the girls went back in the breezeway, trying not to get hit by the bullets that were flying their way. He had finally gotten one of them bitches, and it was the bitch he wanted the most. He heard his goons stop shooting and knew that they ran out of bullets.

"We got to get out of this bitch!" Quick told Savage.

They both wasted no time jumping back in the whip. Before they could peel off, bullets riddled the side of the car with one of the bullets catching Savage in his right shoulder. Being that it was a gated complex they had to wait for the gate to roll open. He knew they were going to make it out because all their attention would be on Kiesha. He looked at his homie, who was taking being shot like the G that he was. He had remembered about the lawyer and Pablo, which he had to put on the back burner now. He couldn't go to the hospital because Detective Stronbone would be all over this shit. He had no choice but to take him to Lovey and Lexi so they could at least pull the bullet out, because going to jail was the last place to go.

He busted a right out of the apartments, made it to W.W. White, then made his way to Springhill. Even though his homie got shot, he was feeling good because he had finally got one of them. At the same time, he knew Babygurl would be hurt due to Kiesha being the only person outside of Kilo that she loved the most. He knew she would turn up the heat, so all he could do was stay prepared and stack as much money as he could, because shit had just got real.

***

It didn't take long for Valerie to get up with Detective Stronbone. She had just pulled into the Budget Suites off of Fredricksberg Road with the intention of doing whatever she had to do to get hm to eat out of her hands. She didn't want to do it, but she wanted Slugga out of jail. It was also becoming addictive to play both sides. She was liking the little movement that Kilo had going on. He was a boss nigga making boss moves from jail, plus Babygurl had shit on lock.

She spotted Detective Stronbone's car as soon as she pulled in and parked right beside it. This would be an easy job for her. Once she saw how he looked at her when he saw her, she knew he was gone. She texted Lexi to let her know that she was meeting up with the detective and would hit her up when she was done. She stepped out and pulled her yoga pants up into her pussy and ass, which revealed she had no panties on. She threw her purse over her shoulder, then walked up to the door. Before she could knock, the door opened.

"Good morning, sexy mama, come on in," he said, then stepped to the side so she could come in.

"And good morning to you too, handsome," she said as she purposely rubbed her ass against dick. She had to admit that he was cute, but she was used to fucking with black people.

She sat on the bed, then looked him in the eyes. For some reason, she felt uncomfortable around him, but shook it off because she had a mission to complete. She studied him as he sat down in the chair at the table in the far corner.

"I know you didn't want me to come all the way over here just for you to sit in the corner."

He said nothing as he just sat there not believing he was sitting in a suite with a young lady as pretty as her. She stood up, walked to him, then sat on his lap. She instantly felt his hard dick and grinded her ass on it.

"You like what I got going on, don't you? You want some of this young pussy?" she whispered in his ear.

"Hell yeah!" He grabbed her, then turned her around so she was straddling his lap. She took off her shirt and her pretty titties popped out. She leaned forward, placing one of her titties at his mouth. He wasted no time as he sucked each nipple like it was his last meal.

"Oh shit!" she moaned.

"What I gotta do to get some of this prime pussy, sexy mama?"

Valerie stood up, then came out of her yoga pants. She knew she had him where she wanted him because his eyes roamed her body as he licked his lips.

"You can get this pussy anytime I want you to have it as long as you do what I say, when I say." She laid back on the bed, then spread her legs wide and started rubbing on her pussy. "But first I want you to come eat this pussy."

Without any talking he walked to the bed then kneeled between her legs. Her pussy was so fat and wet that he wanted to just fuck the shit out of her. He slid his middle finger in her pussy and couldn't believe how tight she was. He had been so caught up in this case that he hadn't had a chance to get any pussy or even see his wife.

"Hell yeah!" she moaned out as she began to rotate her hips on his finger.

He got bold and put two fingers in as his head dipped and he began sucking on her clit.

"Oh, fuck yeah! Shit!"

She didn't think it was gon' be this good and was glad she let him do his thing. He was finger fucking her and sucking on her pussy so good that she tried to climb up the bed. He locked her legs in between his arms, then stuffed his whole face in her pussy.

"Fuck! I'm cum...cum...cumming!" she yelled as her juices squirted all over his mouth and he tried to slurp up every drip that came out. She thought he was finished, but his tongue kept going a million miles an hour. She clamped her legs around his head, clenched the covers on the bed, and prepared herself for another nut. When he felt her leg clench up for the second time, he began sucking on her clit as she let loose once again.

"Damn, sexy mama you got the sweetest pussy I've tasted in a long time," he said as he stood up.

He began taking off his clothes while she scooted of off the bed and stood on her shaking legs. When he was out of his clothes, she looked straight at his dick. It wasn't what she was used to, but she could work with it. She pushed him on the bed, then got between his legs.

"Now remind me, who is running this shit?" she said as she began to jack him off with one hand while she looked him in the eyes.

"You got it, mama. Just put them pretty lips on me," he said.

"Fuck, mama!"

He was enjoying the way she was playing with his dick. She spit on his dick, then sped up. She didn't want to suck or fuck him, so she was going to try her best to satisfy him in a different way.

As if God had heard her, his phone rang. He leaned over, dug in his pants and grabbed his phone. He looked at it and knew that his play time was over and answered it.

"What's up, Chief? I'm kind of busy here," he said as Valerie continued to jack his dick.

"Get to University Hospital now and find out what the hell happened with those young ladies you been investigating."

"All right. Give me a few minutes. I'm right down the street." He hung up.

Valerie saw in his face that he was almost there and she used both hands with a little more spit.

"OH FUCK!" he yelled as he came all over her hands.

"Damn, daddy, you was backed up." She said as he kept busting. "Maybe when you got time, I can give you some of this sweet pussy."

"I can't wait! But right now, I need to get up with this case. I'll call you." He rushed to get dressed, then left out of the door in a hurry.

She got herself together as she smiled to herself because her mission was accomplished. She didn't know what Kilo had planned for the detective, but she had him right where she needed him.

Chapter 17

Babygurl, Cassy, Sadie, and Ladie sat in the waiting room at University Hospital to hear news about Kiesha. Babygurl knew Kiesha would survive because her girl wouldn't let that bitch-ass nigga take her out like that. She sat alone in the corner by herself, lost in her thoughts. Her girls could feel the anger coming from her. They all knew that the only person she loved outside of Kilo was Kiesha, so they knew she would fill the streets with bullets. As soon as Babygurl looked up towards the double doors, the same doctor that took Kiesha to the back was coming out and headed their way. They all rushed him in a hurry to hear the news.

"What's up, Doc? Talk to me? What's goin' on with my sister? Is she gon' make it?" Babygurl asked question after question without giving him a chance.

"Slow down now. Yes, she is going to make it, but she is in critical condition. We removed all of the bullets. If you hadn't brought her in as fast as you did, she wouldn't have made it, so y'all did save her life."

"When can we see her?" asked Cassy.

"Right now, she is resting up. Now, I'm not supposed to be doing this, but I can see how much love you girls have for her. She's in 210. Make it quick." He began to walk off.

Before he got to even take two steps, all four of them gave him a hug at the same time.

"Thank you!" they all said at once.

"You're welcome. Just make sure y'all take care of each other." He smiled, then walked down the hallway.

Without waiting they took off, not even bothering to ask for directions. They found the room in no time, then entered slowly. It hurt Babygurl's heart to see her best friend laid up helpless like she was. Her pain instantly fueled her anger as she stood there and looked at Kiesha. Even though she looked peacefully asleep, she knew her girl was in pain. She grabbed her hand as Cassy grabbed the other and both squeezed them lightly.

"We here, girl. We need you to get strong so we can get back to what we do best. Those bitch-ass niggas caught you slipping, but I promise you, they gon' pay for it," Babygurl said with tears in her eyes.

"Don't worry, y'all, I shot that yella-ass nigga he always with. Next time I hit one of them, it'll be over with for 'em," said Cassy.

Before Sadie or Ladie could say something, someone knocked on the door, which made all of them turn their heads. When they saw Detective Stronbone in the doorway, they all rolled their eyes and shook their heads.

"Let me guess. Y'all ain't happy to see Uncle Stronbone." He laughed at his own joke as he stepped in the room. "I see that Quick finally got one of y'all. I don't know whether to be happy or disappointed. It don't matter either way because when it's all said and done, y'all are either gon' be in prison with y'all boys or dead. So, which one of y'all gon' tell me what happened?"

"She was just an innocent bystander: wrong place, wrong time. Now if you will excuse us, we would like to kick it with our girl," Babygurl said then they all turned back to Kiesha.

"You know, even though I hate y'all with everything I got, I respect y'all. Keep it up, and I'ma have everything I need to slam every last one of y'all. I know Quick did this. I just hope I get you before he does. Better yet, I don't give a damn. Either way, y'all will be off my streets."

"Fuckin pig-ass bitch!" Sadie yelled as he walked out of the room.

As they turned to talk to Kiesha some more, a nurse stuck her head in the door.

"Visit time is up."

"Alright." Babygurl turned back to Kiesha. "It's time for us to go, but we'll come tomorrow."

They all kissed her on the forehead and made a promise one more time to smoke Quick and whoever else rode with him. She had a way to hit Quick where it hurt, and now it was time to put that play in motion.

***

Quick sat in front of Savage spot on Marbach Road waiting on him to come out so they could meet up with Pablo. They were supposed to meet up with him two days ago, but he had gotten at Kiesha, plus one of the hoes shot his homie, so that had delayed shit. He hit the Sweet that he had lit and smiled to himself as he saw how Kiesha went down. He looked towards the house and spotted Savage coming down the steps. His arm was in a sling, but bro was still swaggy. All he could do was shake his head as Savage jumped in the passenger seat.

"Damn, nigga, what took you so long? Let me find out Babygurl and them hoes got you scared to come out and shit." Quick handed him the stick of gas he was smoking.

"Nigga, fuck you! I know you ain't talkin about nobody being scared, talkin' 'bout we need to get out this bitch, soundin like Terry Crews off of *Malibu's Most Wanted* and shit," he said and they both started laughing hard as hell.

Quick pulled off but kept the music down so he could think.

"So, what do you think bro want to where he gotta keep hittin' you up so much? I know we ain't been late or short on the payments," Savage asked, then passed him the Sweet back.

"I don't know. I just hope it's about making some more money, because we sho' gon' need it. We need to be recruiting some more niggas because that bitch Babygurl fa'sho' finna be gunnin' at us now."

"I'm on that now. Shit, she already got damn near half the city ridin' under her, so that shit been tough," Savage said, scrolling through his phone.

"I know Jessica tryna plug me in with her cousins. She say they got a team full of gangstas that's trained to go, but if push comes to shove, I can see if Pablo could help us out."

"Shit, you betta take her up on her offer. Them Mexicans got heart. That's probably why Babygurl 'bout that life."

"Naw, that bitch just crazy. She really a black girl trapped in a Mexican's body, plus she fuck with that nigga Kilo, and he throwed off to the max."

They both stayed quiet after that, so Quick turned the radio up so he could drown out whatever other questions his homie wanted to ask. He remembered when he was first introduced to the squad and some of the gangsta shit they did. He had never seen a squad as loyal as them. He and Correy were down with the movement that the two hustlers had and he was on the way to taking San Antonio over until Correy found out about Babygurl setting up his brother Rico.

He was so lost in his memories that if he hadn't looked up, he would have missed his exit. Stone Oak was a different world to him. He had never been on this side of town, so he had to plug the address that Pablo had given him to the restaurant into the GPS. It had taken him no more than five minutes to find and put in.

"Look at all these white hoes out here," Savage said, looking at the different breed of women than he was used to.

"Real talk."

He found a parking spot, they sprayed some of the red Polo that Quick had on deck, then stepped out. They walked inside, and the smell of Mexican food hit their noses hard. They spotted Pablo sitting alone in the back and headed his way.

"Pablo, my man, what's good?" Quick greeted as they both took seats.

"Mijos, let order some food."

They ordered their food and drinks, then waited for the waitress to leave.

"Have y'all heard of a crew about ten years back called Money Train Mafia?" he said while looking at them both to see their reaction.

"I've heard of 'em, but they ain't making no noise no more. But why you ask?" Quick shot back.

Before he could say something back, the waitress brought out their drinks, and once again, he waited until she left,

"I used to supply a man by the name of Tree. He ran Money Train Mafia and brought me a lot of money until his head got too big for his body. He married a Japanese girl who connected him with her father, and that's when he tried to take my spots. We have been beefing for at least ten years, but a couple of years ago, he slid back so I couldn't find him."

He stopped because the food was being placed in front of him. They dug in before they started back and Savage was the first one to break the silence.

"No offense, but what's that got to do with us?" Savage said as he stuffed his mouth with the enchiladas on his plate.

"I went out this past weekend and I saw Tree chilling in one of the VIP booths after the DJ gave him and ya girl Babygurl a shout out. I wanted to tell my amigos to shut the club down, but they were too deep."

When Quick heard Babygurl's name, he damn near choked on his food. "So you telling me that the squad plugged in with this nigga? I wonder how that happened?" asked Quick confused.

"First off, she's not only connected to him, but through him, she's connected to the Japanese cartel. Second, it happened because he has two twin girls who happen to be a part of Babygurl's squad.

"Sadie and Ladie," said Quick. "Ain't this a bitch!"

"Now I got a proposition for you."

"Talk to me."

"In the process of gunning down ya girl, if you get Tree, I'll give you, Savage, and Correy unlimited drugs, guns, and more connects than you can imagine."

"I don't have the manpower for that right now," said Quick.

"Let me handle that." He smiled, then continued to eat his food.

Now that Quick knew that Babygurl was plugged in with the Japanese cartel, he knew where those Asian hittas came from. She was well-connected, and now it was time for her to see how well-connected he was.

Ray Vinci

Chapter 18

The whole squad was at the spot in the Landings apartment complex, ready for war. She had this little area on smash, so she knew Quick wouldn't show his face. She wanted to smoke Quick so bad that it was killing her. She knew that Kilo would want to be a part of offing him, plus she wanted Correy to feel what Quick would feel. She looked in everybody's eyes to see if they had it in them to take this shit to the next level and all she saw was loyalty. Kilo, Illy, Slugga, and Felony would be home in a few days, so she knew shit was about to get real. She kept checking her phone, waiting on the text to come from Lexi.

They made themselves get along because of Kilo, and due to Bianca just having the baby, she had to deal with her.

"Twan and Li'l, Tony y'all with me. Whenever Lexi shoot me the text to where Quick's li'l bitch is, we snatching her ass up, no questions," Babygurl said, making her point.

"Cool," Twan shot back.

She lit a Newport, then inhaled the smoke as hard as she could. She needed to clear her mind for this mission. It had been a minute since she rode without Kiesha, and the shit was fucking with her head. What was fucking with her the most was the Mexican that Tree was flexed up with in the club this past weekend. She and her squad were ready to light him and the rest of them Mexicans that he was with up, but Tree stopped her. The next day, she called and drilled them about who they were. Yeah, he used to beef with the nigga back in the day, but all she heard was that he was Quick's new connect and the head of the Mexican Mafia. How he did that, she didn't know or care. All she wanted was Correy, Quick, and Savage. It made it even better that Tree put a half a million dollars on Pablo, so his ass had to go to.

She was snapped out of her thoughts by Sean pulling up behind her, placing his arms around her waist, then pulling her tight to his chest.

"You quiet, shawty. What's on ya mind?" he said in her ear.

"I want blood for my homegirl, plus it seems like the more money, the more problems," she said as she finished her cigarette.

"Don't worry, shawty, I got something for the stress."

He grabbed her by the hand, then pulled her to the restroom. As soon as he locked the door, he bent her over the sink, lifted her Fendi skirt, slid her thong to the side, then dove in tongue first.

"Ummm…yes!" she moaned out loudly. She wasn't expecting this, but she needed it.

He stabbed his tongue in and out of her pussy like he was trying to catch a murder case. She put one of her legs on the sink as he spread both of her fat ass cheeks so he could taste every part of her.

"Fuck yeah, baby, eat this pussy. Ssss!"

He knew she was about to cum because her walls started clenching around his tongue.

"OH FUCK! Here it comes!" she moaned as she let loose her juices all over his tongue and chin.

Instead of sucking up her juices, he stood up, pulled his dick out, and slid right in. He had to grip her waist because she tried to run. Once he had a good grip, he long-stroked her until he was hitting the back of her pussy.

"Damn, shawty, this pussy juicy. Fuck!" he groaned as he smacked her ass.

"Daddy you fu-fuckin' the shit!" She couldn't finish because she was busting all over his dick. She started throwing her ass back, taking all eight inches with every thrust. She heard her phone beep and knew that it was time to ride, so she sped up, throwing that ass back. "Fuck this pussy, daddy. Get that nut!" She looked back because that nigga was in her stomach.

"Oh shit! Grrr!" he groaned as he busted inside of her, which made her feel more of him in her stomach.

They got themselves together, then looked at her phone and saw the address.

"Thank you, baby. I needed that bad."

"Let me take Li'l Tony's spot."

"Naw, I'm tryna figure some shit out. I'll let you know what's up when I get the chance. Just get ready. I'll be back in a couple of hours."

Babygurl, Twan, and Li'l Tony loaded up in the brown minivan they had rented from a dopefiend, then headed to Broadway. She rode in the passenger seat while Li'l Tony rode in the back. She wanted him to be the one to snatch her up because he seemed a little different lately.

It took them thirty minutes for them to get to Broadway. She didn't like doing any type of crime so close to the airport, but they had to get at Quick. Once she got to the street where Jessica stayed, Twan parked two houses down from where her house sat.

Jessica stayed in a nice neighborhood with nice houses and cars. Babygurl knew she had to be careful because there were important people that stayed in these parts of the city. She remembered when Correy and Quick had kidnapped her, which pissed her off even more.

"Bitch-ass niggas," she whispered to herself.

"What?" asked Twan.

"Nothin'. Just be ready when she come out."

He looked at her like she was crazy as she set her strap in her lap. She was at ease from the sex she just had. She wanted to top it off with a blunt of kush, but she needed to focus.

"There she go right there!" Li'l Tony said, making her bring her attention back to the house. She was just coming out and locking her door when Twan pulled off at normal speed. Good thing that her car was parked on the street.

"Pull up on her and when I get out, Li'l Tony, get ready," she said with her gun in one hand and the other on the door.

As soon as Jessica put her hand on the door handle, Twan pulled up next to her and Babygurl jumped out with the banga to her head.

"Try to run or make any kind of sound, and I'ma send yo' brains flying back to Mexico," she said through clenched teeth.

"Do you know who my father is?"

Babygurl cocked back and slapped the shit out of her with the strap, knocking her out cold. Before she could hit the ground, Li'l

Tony caught her and pulled her into the van. He was mad because the wound from where Babygurl had hit her was leaking blood all over his Louis Vuitton unit.

Babygurl picked up Jessica's purse, phone, and keys and got back in the van as Twan sped back to the northeast side of town.

***

Kilo, Illy, Slugga, and Felony sat in Kilo's cell blowing a blunt of kush. Ms. Washington had been coming through for him like she promised. All he had to do was keep hitting her off with some dick and in return, he and his homies were living like kings. They had the whole sixth floor sewed up so niggas didn't even think about trying them. Niggas were trying to get with the squad, but only a few made the team. Even though he had put some bread on Correy's head, he wasn't really worried about him because in a couple of days, they would all be back on the streets. He knew that Correy had money on his head, but he ran shit, so that was the least of his worries.

"It's been a long eight months. You ready or what?" Illy asked his big bro ,then hit sweet number two.

"Hell yeah! Bianca just had my li'l nigga, plus Babygurl got shit ready for us."

"I can't wait to put one in that bitch-ass nigga Quick. Nigga got my li'l mama laid up in the hospital with his pussy ass," Slugga said with venom in his voice.

"Don't worry. By the time we done with these three niggas, they gon' wish they never met a nigga in the squad. I done put together some shit that only I could understand." Kilo took the blunt from Illy, then inhaled deep.

"I'm just glad I'm getting out. I need some pussy," added Felony.

"Nigga, you just stressin' who Cassy givin the pussy to," Illy said.

"Nigga, Cassy's ass is locked down. She know betta. But what's up with these Atlanta niggas Babygurl got riding with her?"

"I had Agent Long look into them niggas, and so far, they one hunnid. They been holdin' the girls down, so as long as it stays that way, they good with me."

At first, he was fucked up about Babygurl bringing in some random-ass niggas, and if it wasn't for Bianca vouching for them, he would've made her cut them niggas off. He still kept a close watch on them, so he knew Babygurl was feeling the nigga Sean. Yeah, he was jealous, but he was still top dog and she made sure she let him know that. That was still his ride or die, but Bianca had him on lock, plus Lexi was doing her thang.

"The question is, how did you get Lexi to get right? I thought after Babygurl smoked her sister, shit was a done deal," said Slugga.

"Good dick, my friend. Good dick," he said, and they all started laughing. "Naw, on the cool, I think she realizing she fucked up and that shit with Lisa was her fault. I'm just glad she back, 'cause she playing a major part in all this shit."

"I still don't see how yo' ugly ass got all these bad ass hoes. And they all do whateva you say," Illy shot out.

"Good dick, my friend. Good dick."

They busted out laughing and until final rack up, they planned and plotted, waiting until they got out so they could get back to the money. It was time for them to take over, and Kilo would be damned if Correy stood in his way.

Ray Vinci

Chapter 19

Quick was waiting on Philly, Tidy, and Savage to come through so they could head out to Pablo's spot and he could plug them in with his nephews. If he had to go way to the Southside, he was gon' ride with his homies. Fuck what Pablo was talking about. He knew them Mexicans on the Southside was some gangstas, so he had to be prepared just in case shit didn't go as planned. He had been hitting up Jessica so she could ride out with him, but he never got an answer, so he said fuck it.

He heard a car pull up, making him look out of the front window. When he saw the red Camaro sitting in front of his house, he knew exactly who it was.

He had forgotten he had told her to come to his house so she could drop that bread for get Correy out. He would be home in a few days, so he had to drop that sack off. She was looking sexy as hell in all her all-black Yves St. Laurent business dress that stopped at mid-thigh. It showed off of every curve she had, which made Quick's dick hard as hell. She looked tall in her black Christians with the red bottoms. Her hair hung down to her back, and all Quick could think about was wrapping her shit around his arm.

As she got to the door, before she could knock, Quick opened it. He stared at her and couldn't help but lick his lips.

"Damn, li'l mama, you lookin' good."

"Thank you." She stepped inside. "This can't take long because I have to get back to work."

"Cool. Sit down while I go get it."

Quick walked straight to his room and pulled out five neatly wrapped stacks of hundreds. He was gon' give her extra for making that happen for his homie. He grabbed the small Gucci backpack, then put the stacks in. He secured his safe, threw the bag over his shoulder, then walked back up front.

"My homies should be coming through in like twenty minutes so you can count it before they come if you want to, plus I put a li'l extra on the top for good service." He handed her the bag, then sat next to her.

"No, I trust you. But since we only got twenty minutes, let me see what I felt last time we sat on this couch." She reached over to unzip his pants before he could deny her. He let her go in and pull his dick out. Her eyes got big at what she was holding in her hand as she stroked it to full hardness. "Damn! You got a big-ass dick! Oh my God!" She had to jack him off with both hands while she dipped her head and put his tip in her mouth. She could only get it halfway in her mouth before she felt him in the back of her mouth. She wasted no time sucking his dick with as much spit as she could get while stroking the rest. She was gagging due to her being greedy.

"Fuck, li'l mama! Eat that dick!" he moaned as he put his hand on the back of her head. He let her have her way before he pulled her up. She looked at him like he was crazy but understood when he dragged his pants and boxers to his feet.

"We only got a li'l while until my homies get here, so we ain't got time for that. I'm tryna beat that pussy in."

"Oh, this ain't gon' take long." She pulled her dress over her ass and left it at her waist. She climbed his lap, slid her thong to the side, then sat on the head. He only had the head in and it already felt like he was all the way in.

"OH MY GOD! SHIT!" She started cumming as soon as she started sliding down. "I'm cumming!"

Now it was easier for him to slide in, so he grabbed her waist and pumped in her slow.

"Damn, li'l mama, this pussy tight. I'm finna fuck the shit out of yo' li'l white ass."

She couldn't even say anything as she leaned into him, wrapping her arms around his neck. She didn't realize she made that mistake until he pumped in her a little bit faster.

"SHIT! Fuck me with this big black dick!" she yelled as she felt him in her stomach. The more he pumped, the more she tried to get off of it, but he had his arms locked around her waist.

"I'm cu-cu-cumming again!"

She came again, but she kept riding his shit because even though he paid her, she was still on a mission.

"Oh shit!" was all he could get out because her pussy was wet as hell. "I'm finna make this pussy mine."

He was drilling her shit as he felt her body let loose, which made him shoot a load inside of her.

"Fuck!" they both said at the same time. She bounced a few more times, making sure she got everything out.

"Damn, what I gotta do to keep you on the team?" Quick said, then moved her off his dick.

"I'm already on a team, but maybe we could do something."

She knew she had him already without even giving him any pussy. She just had to fuck him. Even though Quick was a boss in his own right, she was already loyal to the squad.

They both got dressed, then headed for the door. When he opened it to let her out, he saw all of his homies pull up.

"I'ma hit you up," he told her as she got in her Camaro and peeled off.

He slid in Savage's Range Rover. Philly was riding with Tidy while two of his li'l homies were riding behind Tidy. They pulled off to the southside three cars deep.

"You think these niggas gon' try us or what?" asked Savage as he sipped the drink that was in his cup.

"Naw, but we gon' be ready if they do. I wanted to wait for the homie to touch down, but we need these niggas."

"Ain't he steppin' out in like two days?" Savage asked.

"Hell yeah. I'm glad too, because we need my nigga out here runnin' this shit with us."

That's all that was said for the rest of the ride because he needed to concentrate. Savage turned up the 21 Savage that was in his deck, then tuned out himself.

The drive took about twenty minutes with Quick steady glancing in his sideview mirror to make sure Philly, Tidy, and his two li'l homies were still behind them. He lit up a Newport, then texted Pablo to let him know he was down the street. He pulled up in Indian Creek and saw a bunch of Mexicans draped out in blue. He kept driving to what looked to be the middle of the hood. When they pulled up in front of the apartment, Pablo stepped outside with two Mexicans who looked like they were getting to a lot of money.

"Shit, it lookin' like they getting to some bread," said Savage.

"Hell yeah!" Quick shot back, then scoped the hood out. There were a bunch of Mexicans, and he automatically knew they were the only black people present.

"I'm glad we didn't ride out here by ourselves," said Quick.

Pablo waved him to where he was as both he and Savage stepped out, double-checking to make sure they each had they banga in reach. Quick looked back, giving Philly, Tidy, and his li'l homies the go-ahead to step out and follow them. They all walked up to Pablo and he immediately shook his hand, then introduced him to Philly and Tidy.

"Mijo, step inside so we can talk. Too many eyes out here." Pablo then walked back inside of the apartment with the whole team behind him.

When Quick walked inside, he liked what he was seeing. He had all of the apartments in this little block gutted into one. There was money, dope, and guns everywhere, plus five more Mexicans draped in tattoos and jewelry. All five of them stopped what they were doing, eyeing them as they walked in. He knew if Pablo hadn't laced them niggas up, they would've been flexing hard.

"Quick, these are my nephews, Juan and Jose. They run this side of town. Juan, Jose, this is Quick and Savage," Pablo said, introducing them to each other.

They nodded their heads in acknowledgment. Pablo gestured for everybody to sit down, but he stayed standing.

"I got y'all together because as one, y'all can run San Antonio with ease. But y'all have the squad, and now Money Train Mafia in y'all way," he explained. "As all y'all know, both these families are hard to deal with. I want Tree's head on a plate, so if y'all can do that while you getting at Babygurl, y'all have the connect y'all need to become bosses."

"Shit, we all in!" said Quick.

"Shit, us too!" said Juan.

Quick was about to add something else until he felt his phone vibrate in his pocket. He pulled it out and saw Jessica's number flash across the screen and immediately answered it.

"Girl, where the hell you at? I been hittin' yo' shit all day," Quick said calmly.

"If you talkin' about yo' li'l broad, she most definitely not in a good spot right now."

His eyes almost popped out of his head when he heard Baby-gurl's voice on the other end of the phone.

"Where is Jessica!" he yelled through the phone, making him catch the attention of Pablo when he heard his daughter's name.

"Oh, she tied up right now. Can I take a message?" She started laughing.

"Bitch, you don't know what you just did. You just signed your death certificate."

"How about you for her? Or should I fill her pretty ass up with holes like you did my homegirl," she said. "I don't even know what I'm saying. I'm about to do this bitch bad no matter what. You and ya li'l team just need to fall in line because y'all next."

She hung up before he could say something, leaving his adrenaline rushing.

"What the fuck was that about, and who has my daughter Quick?" asked Pablo.

"They got Jessica," was all he could say.

He saw the anger slowly rise in Pablo's eyes, knowing Baby-gurl was about to feel his heat. He wasn't expecting no shit like this, and it was pissing him off that she always had the upper hand on him.

"Go get my daughter, Quick, and bring me that bitch's head along with Tree's." He then walked off to make some calls.

Quick stood up to leave along with his homies. The Mexicans got up and followed him out, ready to tear shit up. He was now where he needed to be to take Babygurl and Kilo out.

***

Correy had just gotten off of the phone with Lovey, letting her know that he was coming home in two days. He was ready to tear the streets up once he touched down. Lovey was all up in his ear about getting out of the game, that he had enough money to be set for the rest of his life. He wasn't trying to hear none of that shit she was talking about. He had too much going for him to leave the game. He understood that she was scared for him, but he couldn't let Kilo and Babygurl live after what they had done to Rico.

He headed straight to his cell due to having a lot of shit on his mind, so he didn't want to be fucked with. Quick had been putting on for the team since he'd been gone, but it was time for him to pick up where he left off. Quick had been putting in work out there, and all he was still hearing was the squad's name. Whatever Kilo had Babygurl doing was working, because she had shit on lock. All that shit was about to come to a stop though. He wasn't about to let them run shit while he has breath in his body.

He had heard Babygurl was plugged in with the Japanese Cartel. He didn't give a fuck who she was plugged in with. Her ass was dead, and whoever stepped in his way of his takeover of San Antonio would be dead with her. No matter what, he was gon' come out on top. He laid back in his bunk, plotting on different ways to take out the squad. He knew it wouldn't be easy, so he kept his mind in plan mode. He continued to think as his eyes drifted close, knowing that even in his sleep, he was dreaming about being king of San Antonio.

Chapter 20

Bianca had been waiting on this day for months, and now it was finally here. Today, Kilo would be stepping out of the county with ten years of deferred probation attached to him. She and Valerie had managed to get all of them ten year deferred probation with the help of their cousin Agent Long altering the documents. She had put together a little get-together to welcome Kilo home. He also wanted to meet up with everybody so he could let everybody know he was home.

She stepped out of the bathroom of hers and Kilo's new house, then walked straight to the closet to find something sexy to wear for her man when he stepped foot out of jail. She decided to keep it simple due to her just having her baby two weeks ago. She chose some khaki Christian Dior short shorts that showed off her ass, thighs, and pussy print. Her purple Dior shirt was tight around her stomach and chest. She chose her purple Christian Dior heels that encased her foot but showed off her toes. She draped her neck, ears, wrists, and fingers in diamonds, then pinned her hair back in a ponytail. She checked herself out in the mirror and was loving what she was seeing. She had dropped the kids off with her parents because she knew what type of night this would be.

She grabbed her Birkin bag, phone, and keys to the brand new smoked grey Lincoln Aviator that Babygurl had copped Kilo as a welcome home gift. Canyon Lake was about a thirty-minute drive from the county jail, so she turned up Summer Walker, then relaxed as she drove to San Antonio city limits.

She thought about Kilo handling the situation with Correy because he was a part of the ten-year probation deal. Just like Kilo, he would be getting out today as well. She knew Kilo wouldn't stop beefing with Correy until one of them was dead. She just hoped Kilo would be the survivor. All Bianca could do was ride with him and make sure shit go right on the legal side. She had seen more money since she had been fucking with the squad than she did within the timeframe of her being a lawyer.

Her phone binged, letting her know she had a text message. She already knew it was Babygurl as she reached for her phone in the passenger seat. She laughed at the text because Babygurl and them were bugging. They had decided to throw the party at Baby Jay's and Sadie's new spot, on Pinn Road.

She pulled up to Bexar County Jail and parked right in front. When the people outside saw the Lincoln Aviator, everybody's eyes locked in on it. This shit seemed like déjà vu to her, so she made a mental note to sit Kilo down to let him know he had to at least slow down.

It felt like forever before Kilo came out in the same clothes he had on the day he got locked up. He still looked fresh in his eight-month-old outfit, plus he had a fresh haircut like he just jumped out of the barber chair. Her heart was beating because her man was sexy as hell and looked just like the boss he was. Her pussy got instantly wet just looking at him. She watched him as he looked around confused, making her laugh at the mug on his face.

She slowly stepped out, looking sexy as all eyes were on the white girl that was stacked like the black girl. She was used to the attention, but the way Kilo was looking at her was a whole different look. She walked as fast as she could in her heels. She jumped right in his arms, wrapping her legs around his waist as he clutched her big-ass booty. She kissed him soft, but she still tried to stuff her tongue down his throat. She'd missed him so much and couldn't wait to ride his dick until she made him tap out.

"Damn, li'l mama, you look good as fuck. Let's get away from this jail before I get at that pussy right here," he whispered in her ear while he walked her to the Aviator.

"I love you, daddy! I missed you so much. You know I can't have you away from me." She looked him in the eyes.

He loved those green eyes and got lost in them quick. "I love you too. And you can tell that I missed you too."

He made her sit on his dick so she could feel how hard he was, then sat her down. She was too excited to react and back up so he could get a good look at the car.

"You living like this since I've been gone? Oh, it gots to be good out here!" He looked inside and was most definitely feeling the peanut butter guts.

"No, it's how you living. Babygurl bought you this as a welcome home gift."

He looked at her with a big smile on his face. Fresh out, and he was already feeling what was ahead.

"Oh, just wait, it's a whole lot of shit to welcome later on. Let's go get you out of these old-ass clothes so you can go meet your squad."

He said nothing as he walked around to the driver's side and got in while she slid in the passenger seat He scanned through the playlist, settled on some Moneybagg Yo, then pulled off.

"So where to?" he asked.

She tapped the Canyon Lake address into the GPS, then leaned back to enjoy his presence that she missed so much. He bobbed his head to the music, wishing he had something to smoke on. Even though he was enjoying the silence, he was the first to break the silence.

"So, when do that nigga Correy get out?"

"Sometime today."

"Tell Valerie I got something for her for everything. She playing her part like she was born for this shit. When do my homies get out?" he asked.

"Tomorrow or the day after that. We made sure all the paperwork went through before we left the courthouse. You know we got your back, plus Babygurl been holding it down for the squad. I can tell she learned from you. I swear, that girl is like the female version of you."

"Yeah, she did her thing, but I'm most proud of you. You handled yo' business. You rode for me non-stop and made sure I had the right connects that I needed to start an empire. You the best, li'l mama, and I'ma make sure you ain't gotta go through this shit no more," he said as she stayed quiet. "I can't wait to meet my li'l boy and see my daughter."

They rode for the rest of the ride as she caught him up on everything he needed to be laced with. They were in front of the Canyon Lakes mansion in no time. He was loving the way he was living as he made his way inside to get ready to meet up with his squad and party so he could start his movement to the top.

***

This spot had proved to be worth every last one of Quick's homies that she had to body just to get it. Baby Jay and Sadie were doing numbers out of this bitch, and she as loving every bit of it. Everybody was there waiting on Bianca and Kilo to show up. Even though Babygurl was fucking with Sean, she knew she would never stop loving Kilo. She did respect what he and Bianca had, so she would play her part as his ride or die. She was dressed in some blue jean Dolce and Gabbana skinny jeans and a white Dolce and Gabbana halter top that showed off her breasts, and white and black retro 12s for just in case some shit popped off. She had Tiffany's diamonds that shined on every part they were at. She let her hair hang down to her ass, which was fat as hell in those skintight pants.

She spotted the Lincoln Aviator that she had copped for Kilo and her heart sped up. She was ready to crown this nigga the king of the squad. She had been waiting on this moment for almost a year. She knew that with Kilo back on the scene, shit was about to get ten times more gangsta for Quick.

Kilo stepped out looking good in his brand-new khaki Gucci shorts with the red and green stripe going down the side. His matching shirt felt snug against his chest and white tee. He had on some khaki Gucci loafers with no socks. His jewelry was compliments of one of Tree's Asian connects. Diamonds sparkled from his ears, neck, wrists, and fingers, and it somehow made his fresh haircut stand out. He walked up to Babygurl and hugged her tight. She started crying instantly because she had built all this for him, and now he was finally home to take this shit to the next level.

"I'm here now, li'l mama. I got you. Now let's go handle business." He put his arm around her shoulder, then they stepped inside to greet the rest of the squad.

When he stepped in, there were niggas and bitched packed inside of the apartment with just enough room to move. Cassy, Sadie, and Ladie all screamed as they ran to give him a group hug. Yeah, they had Sean and his family, but it was nothing like having Kilo, Illy, Slugga, and Felony around. They also missed Low Key and Mr. Lee, who had gotten gunned down by one of Correy's hittas.

"We missed you, nigga!" they all almost yelled in unison.

"I missed y'all too. I like the way y'all held down the squad while we was gone. I appreciate everything y'all put work in for. Now it's time to take this shit to the next level." He looked up and made eye contact with a group of niggas he already knew were Sean and his people by the head nods they were giving him. He had planned to pull them to the side whenever he had he time because he needed to see how they were feeling about him coming home and taking over shit.

"Look out! Look out!" he yelled to get everyone's attention. "A lot of you niggas don't know me because me and the rest of the niggas who started this has been locked up for the past eight months. Babygurl and her squad been holdin' shit down, but without y'all's help, none of this would be happening, so thank y'all. Now just because I took over doesn't mean shit about to change. Prices and weekly drops stay the same. This nigga Quick got my li'l sister laid up in the hospital, and I ain't feeling that shit at all. Once everything is situated with me and the homies, we at them niggas' necks. But for now, we party. Y'all enjoy y'all selves, and from me, welcome to the squad."

Everybody cheered and was finally happy that the bossman was home. Before he got to mingling with people, Babygurl had given him two brand new Glock 9's so he wouldn't be naked. He tucked them both, then waved Valerie and Lexi over. He sat at the kitchen table with all the girls seated around him. He was surrounded by bad bitches that were about their business. He laced them up about Illy, Slugga, and Felony coming home, and they were all happy.

"I want to introduce you and the boys to somebody tomorrow," said Babygurl.

"Yeah, he been waiting on you to come home so he could meet you," said Sadie.

"That's a bet."

He grabbed a bottle of 1942 and a blunt and enjoyed himself. He was relaxed as he chopped it up with everybody, because after tonight, playtime was over. He loved what Babygurl had put together, which made him promise that when all the beef was over, he had something for them. He was fresh out and having fun.

He hit the blunt and the bottle and prepared for a long night.

Chapter 21

Correy had been out for only seven hours and was already dressed in all black, ready to ride. Quick and Savage had tried to throw him a little welcome home party, but he said that he was good. He, Quick, Savage, Juan, Jose, and a mix of niggas and Mexicans were sitting in a ducked-off spot Quick had right around the corner from Pinn Road. Babygurl had been hitting all his spots lately, slowing his cash flow down. Somebody on his team was giving up info, and he planned to find out pretty soon. He had gotten the call from Savage's li'l cousin letting him know that Babygurl was throwing a little welcome home party for Kilo.

He had caught Kilo slipping on his first night out and was gon' take advantage of it. Correy knew Quick was ready for war because there were at least twenty niggas strapped up. Quick had managed to link up with the southside Mexicans, who didn't give a fuck about nothing but getting their cousin Jessica back. He made a mental note to ask Quick to lace him up on what was going on with that. They all loaded up in van, then headed around the corner. It was a short ride, but Correy wanted to get a feel of the area just in case shit didn't go their way. Even though he knew he caught Kilo and his squad slipping, he respected his gangsta enough that he was still ready to ride at any given minute.

When they got to the apartments, they parked not too far down the way from Quick's old spot. They could see what looked to be a whole army of niggas and bitches out front. He spotted Kilo and Babygurl posted on the porch like shit was sweet.

"Y'all leave them two for me," he told Quick and Savage while pointing at Kilo and Babygurl. He re-checked both his straps as the whole team stepped out of the vans with their guns, ready to bust.

Quick gave the signal for two of his hittas to air that bitch out. It seemed like Kilo felt something was gon' happen and locked right in on them as soon as they let them Draco bullets fly their way. Kilo grabbed Babygurl, then dove back into the hallway. Correy watched as the young goons showed no mercy on the triggers as body after body dropped. Once they both ran out of bullets, Correy wasted no time in letting his trigger finger work, sending sparks flying towards where Kilo was. Quick and Savage were right next to him, putting in work, popping shit left and right. The Mexicans didn't play as they went to work in the opposite direction. Correy liked the way they handled their business, watching them litter the apartments with gun shells.

Out of nowhere, the li'l homie that was next to Quick got riddled with choppa shells, making him dance on the way to the ground. Cassy, Sadie, and Ladie were already knocking shit off one by one when Kilo and Babygurl came back out busting their straps, making them duck behind the vans. Bullets rocked the van side to side, but Correy was too much of a gangsta to panic. He still heard gunshots, but the ones that were coming their way had stopped. He and Quick raised up and rounded the van quickly, letting loose on their triggas. Savage was a little slow due to him just being shot but was still there with them on his best gangsta shit. They watched as their li'l homies kept dropping left and right and realized it was time for them to get out before they ended up smoked.

Correy saw the Mexicans running back their way and that's when he knew that there were too many of these niggas. He noticed that the Mexican's little group of shooters came back short too. A group of niggas with dreads and some nigga that looked like them damn twins came around the corner sending what looked like fireworks their way. He reloaded, then started back busting at the apartment.

"Let's get out this bitch before the rollas come!" yelled Quick over the gunshots.

Correy silently agreed as he jumped in the passenger side of the van. Quick and Savage climbed in the side, then Quick jumped in the passenger side, backing out as fast as possible. Quick looked over at Correy and he had a big-ass smile on his face. All he could do was laugh as he sped out of the apartment dead last while bullets shattered the windows.

Correy was glad he struck blood letting him know that he was still at that bitch Babygurl's head for offing his homie. He was glad to be getting out this bitch alive. Babygurl and Kilo had this bitch looking like Iraq in no time. They had this spot sewed up, and Correy couldn't wait until the next time he got at Kilo. He promised himself that one of them had to go, and it wouldn't be him.

***

Kilo was pissed off about how Correy had hit him up on his first day out. Even though they had his bitch-ass running at the end, it still didn't sit right with him. He wanted to clap back ASAP, but Babygurl said she had something better in mind that would hurt Quick a little more than what he had in mind. Whatever it was Babygurl had planned, they needed to hurry up and get it done because he had to be ready for when his homies got out at 2:00 p.m. He was glad that his squad was out so he could take it to them niggas' heads. He also had to meet with Tree, who he found out was Sadie and Ladie's old man, but he wasn't gon' do that until his squad was by his side.

Babygurl drove him to a dirt road that led to a rundown warehouse that looked like it was barely standing. He spotted Cassy, Sadie, and Ladie plus Sean, Baby Jay, Li'l Tony, Rob, and Twan posted up, waiting for them to pull up.

"Gurl, what type of shit you got going on?" he asked.

"You'll see when you get inside. Let's just say karma's a bitch in the form of Babygurl."

She laughed and he laughed with her. He missed her and was happy to be riding shotgun with her.

"I'm liking how you got them chains iced out too," he said, eyeing everybody's Squad Up chain.

They got out and the whole squad showed them love. He had no problems moving right in as boss. They all respected him like he had never been away from the streets. He and Babygurl were the first to walk into the dark warehouse. She hit a series of light switches, making the whole warehouse light up. He instantly saw a slim Mexican girl tied up in a chair ass naked. He looked at her confused, wondering who the girl was, but understood why she said that karma was a bitch in the form of her. They walked to the middle of the warehouse, then stood right in front of her.

"Why she tied up like this?" asked Kilo.

"Let's see why." Babygurl removed the duct tape roughly, but li'l mama kept it G. "Answer the question, bitch."

"You must not know who my papa is, because if you did, you——"

Before she could finish her sentence, Babygurl backhanded the shit out of her. "I don't give a fuck about ' daddy. All I want to know is where Quick is hiding his dope and money."

"Oh shit! Now I know where I remember you from. You the bitch that Quick wants to kill. You know you's a dead bitch walking," she told her in Spanish, which made Babygurl throw a flurry of punches to Jessica's face, causing her to slump in the chair. Babygurl instantly started kicking her in the stomach. By the time she was done, Jessica was coughing blood. Seeing that Babygurl was handling the situation out of revenge, Kilo stepped in.

"Sadie, Ladie, pick her up," he said, then waited. When they got a better look at her, they immediately recognized who she was. "Li'l mama, I admire yo' gangsta, but you ain't in no position to be bumpin' ya lips. All we want is the stash houses and we'll let you go," Kilo said.

"You wasting your time with her. Why don't you come fuck with a real Mexican mami. You too fine for her."

Kilo laughed at her remark, but stopped once he heard a gun cock. To his surprise, it wasn't Babygurl; it was Sean. When he put it to her head, Kilo just backed up because he could feel that bro was about that life.

"Play with her now and see what happens." Babygurl went and stood next to him.

Kilo had a smirk on his face because he was the same way. She must've known that Sean wasn't playing because she shut up and sat still. He gave Sean a look of approval, then started back up.

"Since you kick it with that bitch-ass nigga, we know you know who his plug is. Just tell us who he is."

She was about to speak but was cut off by Sadie.

"Pablo," she said. "The head of the Mexican Mafia. And this is little Jess, his daughter."

"Well, well, well, Babygurl done hit the jackpot. We got the plug's daughter and Quick's bitch all wrapped up in one present. Welcome home, Kilo." He looked at his watch.

"You got saved today. I gotta go get my homies, but then again, we got all the time in the world. Just don't die on me." He walked off.

Babygurl was right behind him as they jumped in the car. He was already gon' be late, but he was glad that he listened to Babygurl because what was in that warehouse was worth a million bucks. He also knew that this little street war had just become bigger than what it was.

Ray Vinci

Chapter 22

Detective Stronbone was sitting inside of the Skyline Motel. His informant had told him to meet up here because it was closed off so nobody could see him from the road. Personally, he didn't give a fuck where they met up at, or who saw them. He just needed what he had. For the most part, he hated dealing with snitches. Even though they helped, some of them played stupid at the end of it all. He knew his informant wouldn't get on the stand, so he at least had to try and get him to wear a wire. He knew that the odds of him even wearing a wire were slim to none. He already had enough to pin ten years on Kilo's whole squad and Correy's little crew. Whatever he had planned he needed to do it fast because of them starting to get connected.

He was starting to get pissed off because he'd been waiting for an hour and a half. As soon as he was about to pick up his phone to call and talk shit, he spotted the familiar black BMW pull in. He watched with envy as the BMW backed in next to him, but instead of waiting for him to get out, Stronbone got out, then jumped in the passenger seat without waiting for an invitation. He didn't give a fuck about him being pissed off about just jumping in his shit.

"Listen to me, you black piece of shit, I run this shit, so when I give you a time and place, you get your black ass there when I say!" he said in his face as spit flew at him.

"Naw, you look, pig-ass cracker! You need me. The li'l shit I got jammed for I can do time for. I'm just helpin' you out because yo' pig ass lookin' like you about to kill ya'self if you don't get Babygurl. Stupid muthafucka," he added just for the fuck of it to piss him off, then he leaned back and hit his Newport.

It was fucking with him how he got involved with the no good-ass Detective. He had gotten pulled over for running a red light, and the police that pulled him over just so happened to be him. He'd gotten caught with a brick of powder, a gun, and $25,000 cash. He wasn't stressing about doing time; he just didn't want to do Fed time, so he chose to cooperate with the detective.

"Whatever. Just tell me what you got for me, and it better be useful, because I'm so close to just throwing your black ass in jail."

"Well, for starters, Kilo's been out for about four days and as of yesterday, his squad is too. Second, Correy is out and they just had a shootout their first day out. I'm still tryna find out who is supplying them, but Babygurl holdin' that close to her chest. Only her, the girls, and Kilo and his squad know that. And as far as you throwing me in jail, I highly doubt that. I got some valuable information that concerns your well-being. Just give me a li'l bit so I can get some more insight on it."

When he heard everything he'd just told him, it pissed him off. How the fuck did they all get out of jail like that? They were getting too well-connected on both sides. It really ran him hot when he said he had information concerning his well-being.

"Find out what you can, then get back at me," he said, then he got out and slammed the door.

He had to find out what Kilo had up his sleeve before it was too late. He sped out of Skyline Motel with his mind on survival mode. He headed straight home to make sure his wife was okay because with the way Kilo was moving, anything was possible.

***

Kiesha had been laid up for almost two weeks and she was ready to get out of this nasty-ass hospital. The doctor said she would be released at 12:00 p.m., but here it was 1:30 p.m. and Babygurl still hadn't showed up. All she thought and dreamed about was killing Quick's bitch ass. She wasn't expecting him to catch her slipping like that. Babygurl wouldn't let nobody come visit her but Cassy, Sadie, and Ladie. She knew that Kilo, Illy, Slugga, and Felony were out, which made her mad because she missed Slugga just as much as Babygurl and Cassy missed Kilo and Felony. She would still be out of commission for a few weeks due to her arm being in a sling and barely being able to walk. She couldn't get up and get at Quick when she wanted to and that shit irritated her.

"Where the fuck is this bitch at?" she asked herself as she reached to grab her phone off the side table to call Babygurl. She dialed her number, but before she got an answer, Babygurl was standing in the doorway.

"Damn, yo' ass is impatient, calling a bitch out her name and shit," Babygurl said with a grin on her face.

"About damn time. They got me ready to go and you taking yo' sweet-ass time."

"You act like you ain't gon' be doin' the same thing at home that you was doin' here."

"I'm not. Slugga at home and I'm tryna see what that dick do."

"Nasty-ass li'l girl."

Kiesha sat up as the nurse came in with a wheelchair and some crutches. They both helped her into the wheelchair, making her feel helpless. It took them all of fifteen minutes for them to sign the discharge papers and make it down to the emergency door. The car was parked right in front of the doors so when she saw Slugga standing next to Cassy, she damn near jumped out of the wheelchair.

"Daddy!" she yelled as she stood slowly.

"What's up, li'l mama? Damn, a nigga missed the shit out of you." He gave her a hug, making sure not to hurt her, but still gripped two hands full of ass. He tongued her down, making her pussy leak instantly. She grinded on him and felt his dick poking her stomach.

"I hope that pussy ain't out of commission. Crutches or not, I'm still tearing ya red ass up."

"You ain't said nothin'," she shot back.

"Alright, enough of that freaky shit. Let's get up out of here before Kilo sends out a search team." Cassy helped Kiesha into the front seat. Once Slugga and Cassy were situated in the backseat, Babygurl pulled off slowly. She reached to cut the music up, but Kiesha stopped her. Knowing why she did it, Babygurl didn't trip. Babygurl prepared herself for the questions.

"So what's up with Quick?"

"Don't even worry about that nigga. Let me handle that," Slugga said before Babygurl could answer her.

"Nigga, you ain't the one he shot, so you can miss me with that bullshit, li'l daddy."

He looked at her like she was stupid. "Just because yo' ass on crutches don't mean I won't tax that smart-ass mouth."

She was about that life, but she knew not to test his gangsta. Babygurl knew that shit was about to get out of hand, so she cut in.

"I got somebody you can take yo' anger out on," said Babygurl.

"And who might that be?" she asked with irritation in her voice.

"Do you remember the night of my birthday when we seen that nigga in the club?" Kiesha thought back to that night. "Well, that li'l pretty Mexican bitch he was with is his main boo thang. I got her ass tied up waiting on you."

Even though she didn't respond, she had a big-ass smile on her face. Babygurl knew that she had evil shit running through her mind. Wasn't no way in hell she was gon' let her girl sit up while they had all the fun. She knew exactly what Kiesha needed. She raised her console, pulled out a Sweet of kush, then handed to her. She set fire to one end so quick that they all laughed. She hit it like she had been smoking for the two weeks she was in the hospital. Her lungs embraced the smoke easy.

As soon as she went to exhale, the back of the car got riddled with bullets. Slugga and Cassy slid down in the backseat, while Kiesha tried to duck as best as possible. Babygurl ducked low, hit the gas, and was lucky no cars were at the intersection because she ran a red light.

On instinct, Slugga and Cassy pulled out their straps. Wasn't no way they were gon' be able to bust back due to all the bullets coming their way.

"Kiesha, grab the strap in the console!" Babygurl yelled out.

Kiesha wasted no time reaching for the gun. Slugga raised up once Babygurl got a good distance away, trying to get a good look at who was dumping on them. He thought it was Quick, but when he looked in the black Cadillac, he saw some niggas he didn't know. But Slugga knew they were under Quick and Correy.

"Slow down, Babygurl, so they can catch up. Make sure they get on this side. Kiesha, be ready to let loose as soon as they get on the side of us."

Babygurl switched lanes, then slowed down as he and Kiesha got ready. Slugga peeped out of the back window and saw the black Cadillac speeding up on the side of them. Kiesha had to be looking out of the rearview mirror because as soon as they got on the side of them, they both raised up recklessly, squeezing their triggers. Glass shattered as they both continued to bust. Cassy raised up, hoping to get a shot off, but Kiesha and Slugga were handling their business. The Cadillac had bullet holes the size of quarters in it. Both Slugga and Kiesha ran out of bullets at the same time, but the car veered off to the side and rammed into a pole. When they heard the car slam into the pole, their heartbeats slowed down. Babygurl hit the block, then smashed toward the freeway. They were too close to downtown, so she had to get away soon as possible.

Correy had sent some goons their way again and lost. It was their turn to show him what gangsta really was.

Ray Vinci

Chapter 23

Correy, Quick, and Savage had decided to go out to the strip club since they hadn't had any fun since Correy had been home. He was gon' throw his nigga a welcome home party, but Correy quickly shut that idea down. He knew that he couldn't let Kilo catch him slipping like that. Since Correy had touched down, they had been sending that hot shit to the squad left and right. Correy was happy that he took Juan and Jose's offer to go out. He had never been to XTC's Strip Club, so he never realized how bad these Mexican hoes were. He looked over at Quick and saw in his homie's eyes that he was fucked up behind Jessica.

Correy had never met Jessica, but the way she had his homeboy stressed out, he could tell she was one hunnid. He told himself he would help get her back as soon as possible. He thought back to when he and Quick had kidnapped Babygurl. They had beat her ass bad, starved her, and beat her ass some more. Now he understood why Quick was stressed out. If it wasn't for the bitch-ass twins, they would've got everything they wanted out of Babygurl. He turned the bottle of Ciroc up as he snapped back to reality.

His eyes focused on the Mexican girl that was on stage popping her ass in front of them. He had his snapback low, but they still managed to lock eyes with each other. Li'l mama was stacked to the fullest, which made his dick hard while he watched her seduced him and his homies. They all showered her with twenties and fifties as she shook her ass to the music. She seemed to be paying more attention to Correy than the rest of his team. He started to get paranoid, but realized he was on the southside. He stood up, then walked to the stage so he could have her undivided attention. She stood up as well and then shook her ass right in his face. He couldn't help but smack that ass, then stuff some cash in her thong.

She squatted down and leaned into him so she could whisper in his ear. "What's yo' name, papi? I ain't never seen you around here," she said, still moving to the music.

"You never seen me around here because I'm not from around here, and right now my name is not important," Correy shot back.

"If your name is not important, what is?"

"This money."

"Then how about I give you a private session?"

He told Quick the play and for him to watch his back. He stood up as she got off the stage, then followed her to the back. He watched her ass jiggle the whole way and couldn't believe how fat it was. He was ready to see what that pussy felt like.

They walked to the first room, then closed and locked the door. He sat down on the couch that was in there, then laid his pistol next to him. He looked at her to see her reaction, and when she gave no worries to the gun, he leaned back. The music started playing and she began to move her body to the beat. He had begun to relax as she straddled his lap, enjoying the way she was grinding on his dick. She wrapped her arms around his neck and leaned into his ear.

"Damn, you got a big dick. I ain't never fucked no black dude before," she said in his ear over the loud music.

"It's a first time for everything." He slid her thong to the side and stuffed his middle finger all the way in. Her pussy was so wet, the juices ran into the palm of his hand.

"Oh shit," she moaned low in his ear while she bounced slowly on his finger. She was wrapped tightly around his finger, so he knew that she wasn't gon' have a problem when it came to dancing on his dick like she was doing on stage.

He raised her up, then unbuckled his B.B. Simon belt and in one motion, slid everything down to his ankles. She quickly sat back down on the tip but had to slow down due to his thickness.

"OH, MY FUCKING GOD!" she said as she only got halfway down. Her pussy was busting already with her juices flowing down his dick.

As soon as he started pumping in her, he felt his phone vibrate at his ankle. He was gon' let it go, but it had to be important. He slid her off of his lap, then reached down below and grabbed his phone out of his pocket. When he saw that it was Quick, he wasted no time answering.

"Playtime over with. Kilo just hit one of the spots," Quick said before he could even get a word out.

"I'm on my way out right now." He hung up. He hurried up and got himself together, then gave his phone number to ol' girl. He was out of the room faster than he came in, but his mind was no longer on having fun. It was on revenge.

***

Kilo, Illy, Slugga, and Felony sat in one of his old trap spots in New Light Village with Sean, Baby Jay, Li'l Tony, Rob, Twan, and his four Asian hittas. They were counting up the money from the lick they had hit on Correy and Quick's spot last night. Lexi had been hitting him every chance that he got. He was going to split everything down evenly with his squad, but he was gon' give his cut to Lexi along with some more cash. He had told all of the niggas in the squad to meet up here so he could get a good feel for them, plus he was meeting up with Agent Long for some important information. He was liking the way Sean and his boys got down, plus Twan and his killas were some shit to be reckoned with. He knew he had a stomp down team, and that made him wanna ride even more on Correy's and Quick's bitch asses. Babygurl had done good putting the squad up on the next level while he was locked up. Kilo knew he had the game on lock, but Correy was the only nigga in his way of fully taking over San Antonio. He looked at his team and smiled to himself as he inhaled the kush blunt that he had been smoking.

"I ain't gon' lie, that nigga Quick must've been getting to the money, because this is ova $275,000 dollars," said Slugga as he took his cut, then stuffed it in his Louie backpack.

"I wish we knew where his main stash spot was at so I could go 'head and push his wig back," Kilo added, then hit the Sweet again.

"I know," said Illy.

"Oh, don't worry, I got somebody on that, so it's just a matter of time. I know this white boy needs to come on so we can get this shit ova with," Kilo said as he looked at his phone for the first time. They had been waiting on Agent Long for three hours to show up, and it was starting to piss him off.

He was just about to look through his phone for his number when he heard a car pull up in the back. When he looked out of the window, he saw Agent Long stepping out of his car. Kilo smiled to himself because Agent Long most definitely looked out of place. He watched as Agent Long walked up to the back door, but he never had the chance to knock because Felony was opening the door to let him in. Agent Long stepped in and looked around because out of all of them, Kilo was the only one of the squad that he'd never seen in person. Now that he was in their presence, he could feel the gangsta shit that was in them.

"What's up Agent Long? What was so important that we been waitin' three hours for when we could've been gettin' to the money?" Kilo asked as he poured up a cup of drank.

"My bad, I got stuck in a meeting, but for the little information I got, you're going to be glad you waited. Even though it ain't much, I know it's much-needed intel," said Agent Long.

"Well, talk to us. Don't leave us in suspense."

"I know that Detective Stronbone has been dead set on getting y'all off the streets for the past few years, so I started looking at all of his filed paperwork that he had on y'all. He's been pissed because even though he knows y'all got the streets on fire, he has no physical evidence to put any of y'all in jail. As I kept looking, I came across some disturbing shit. No name was listed, but it looks like Detective Stronbone has himself a confidential informant." He looked around the room to see who gave what reaction to what he had just said. When nobody gave anything away, he looked at Kilo as Kilo watched for everybody's reaction just like he did.

When Kilo heard that that bitch-ass detective had a snitch floating around somewhere in his squad giving up info, it made his blood boil. He knew for sure that Illy, Slugga, and Felony were good, plus Babygurl and the girls were solid. Kilo eyed Sean and his fam, then Twan and his killas, and knew that it had to be one of them. He smirked lightly because once he found out which one of them it was, it would be the last time one of them got to run their mouths again.

Agent Long went over to Kilo and whispered in his ear. "We need to find out who is giving up intel that only a selective few should know. Not only will they bring your squad down, but Bianca, Valerie, and me as well," Agent Long said in a very low tone. "Regardless, I'm going to find out who it is, but it's gonna take a few weeks, and we might not have a few weeks."

"Don't worry. When I narrow it down, I'ma get back at you ASAP so you can confirm the person and we can get rid of his snake ass!" Kilo replied in an equally hushed tone while making eye contact with everybody in the room.

"Well, you do that while I go do some more digging."

He stood up, then left out of the back door.

Kilo was in his own world as he plotted on a way to flush the snake out. Kilo realized that if it wasn't one thing, it was another. The more money, the more problems. One thing he knew for sure was that he had made it too far for a member of his own team to take him out. He hit his drink as he wondered how shit got to this point so fast.

Ray Vinci

Chapter 24

Lexi and Lovey were sitting in the living room on the floor, counting up the blue faces that were neatly stacked in front of them. Since they had started doing runs for Quick, the money was piling up faster than they could count. Once they had finished counting up the money they had made with this latest drop, they each profited $15,000. As they stuffed Quick's money in the duffle bag, the front door opened and Correy and Quick walked in. She remembered when she used to be nervous every time she was around them, but now she was good. Now that she was back good with Kilo, she felt like she was kicking it with the enemy. Nobody knew what she had going on with her baby daddy, not even Lovey, and for some reason, she felt like she was being grimy towards her sister.

Correy and Quick said nothing as they walked straight to the back. Lexi watched as they went in the room, which made Lovey look at her sideways.

"What's up with you and Quick? It seems like y'all don't even fuck with each other no more," Lovey asked while lighting a Sweet.

"I don't know. All he seems to be worried about is getting up with Kilo."

"Them niggas on some straight renegade shit."

Lovey passed the Sweet as she thought about the type of shit them niggas was on. She had gotten to the point to where she didn't give a fuck about what they had going on as long as she and Lexi were out of their way. They had already lost their baby sister to the bullshit, so neither one could afford another loss.

Before they could pick the conversation back up, Correy and Quick walked back out, then sat on the couch.

"How much money in that bag?" Quick asked Lexi as he gave her a look that she didn't too much like.

"A li'l bit over $100,000." She pushed the duffle bag his way.

"Oh, y'all hustlin' like that? Shit, I need to be ridin' with y'all then, Joe," Correy said, being sarcastic.

Lexi caught the weak humor then looked from him to Quick. She saw how they were both staring at her and she started to get nervous. She hit the blunt to hide it because she had a feeling that they kind of knew she was playing both sides.

"Shit, we need to be kickin' it with y'all the way y'all got the streets jumpin'," Lovey jumped in and said.

"Kilo the one that got the streets sewed up, no doubt about that. Shit, it seem like since he been home, our money done slowed down drastically. I'm startin' to think that nigga got some kind of intel on my spots because our shit been getting hit left and right," Quick added.

Lexi stayed quiet because now for sure she knew that they knew she was playing both sides. She couldn't even look him in the eyes as she looked at her phone for a distraction. She had to do something to get the focus off of her, so she spoke up.

"You need to find out who it is, because if yo' money slows down, that means mines do to."

He said nothing back to her comment, and she was glad that he didn't. Quick was feeling himself a little too much now that he was on top, and she hated that shit with everything she had in her. It didn't make it better now that Correy was out. Lexi had to admit that them niggas was some bosses, but Kilo was a top-notch boss, so neither one of them could match his hustle or gangsta.

It seemed like hers and Quick's phones rang at the same time, breaking the silence. She saw that it was Kilo then pressed ignore, because she knew not to answer it while these two crazy-ass niggas were in her face. From the smile that appeared on Correy's face, he knew what was going on. He nodded his head slightly but said nothing.

"Come on, gangsta, Savage just got the drop from the plug," Quick said as they both stood up to leave. "Lexi, we gon' link up in a bit, so be ready."

They left, and she let out a deep breath. She was glad that Lovey was oblivious to what was going on, even though she hated not telling her sister what was going down with her. She kicked it with Lovey for a few more hours, then made her way to the Eastside to meet up with Kilo.

***

Babygurl and Kiesha sat outside of the warehouse where they had Jessica stashed for the last three weeks. She had been back and forth trying to get her to give up Quick's stash spot, but she gave up nothing. Babygurl had to admit that Jessica had heart, and if she wasn't riding with the enemy, she would've put her on with her squad. Kiesha, who was walking better, was fed up with waiting on her to give up the info that they wanted and was ready to smoke her, but Kilo shut that down because Tree wanted Pablo dead or alive.

She knew that Pablo had put a price on their heads as well, so they had to move accordingly. She and Kiesha stepped out, then made their way inside of the warehouse. Jessica was still tied up in the middle, ass naked and a few pounds lighter due to her not having eaten much since being there. This time she had brought her some Taco Bell because she didn't need her dying before they got what they needed. When they stood in front of her, Kiesha cocked back and slapped the shit out of her.

"Wake up, bitch," Kiesha said as Jessica's head jerked to the side.

Her face was swollen due to the beatings Kiesha gave her every time they came.

"Bitch, you lucky I don't want you to die on us before I get what I need. Now I was nice enough to bring you some food, so when I untie you, if you do anything stupid, yo' brain will decorate this concrete," Babygurl said as she set the tacos on her lap, then went to untie her.

Kiesha put her strap to her head as Jessica's hands came from behind the chair and attacked her food. Babygurl smiled to herself because she was stuffing the food in her mouth and choking as she tried to swallow it. It took her no time to finish the food as Babygurl gave her the drink, then watched her down it just like she did the food. Once she was done, Babygurl tied her back up.

"So what's up? You ready to give this nigga stash up or what? Because from the looks of it, Quick ain't even puttin' no effort into finding you." Babygurl said while kneeling in front of her.

"I ain't telling you shit, so you might as well kill me, because once my papa finds you, you're dead," she said in a hoarse voice due to days of having no water.

"You know what?" Babygurl went in her back pocket and pulled out a phone, which Jessica knew was hers. "Let's see what ya daddy gots to say." She held the phone to her ear, but it didn't take long for her to get an answer from the other end. "Hello, Papa," she said with an accent.

"Where is my daughter? Give her up and I will give you a head start getting out of Texas!" Pablo yelled through the phone in Spanish.

"First off, blame Quick for this shit. Now I'll make you the deal of a lifetime. Tell Quick to come holla at me if he wanna see his boo thang again. And seeing that Tree ain't too fond of you and wants yo' head on a platter, you should consider that too, if you want to see your li'l baby again," she said in Spanish, then hung up. "Let's see if they really love yo' li'l pretty ass, because if not, next time you see me will be your last breath."

She and Kiesha walked off, leaving her just like she was when they came.

Babygurl was done playing games with Quick, and he was about to find out sooner rather than later.

Chapter 25

The money was coming in at a fast pace, but Kilo had shut down all of his traps so he could address the problem that Agent Long had told him about. He'd be damned if he let some snitch-ass nigga come take down what they started from the mud. Illy, Slugga, Felony, Kiesha, Cassy, Sadie, and Ladie was seated next to each other in the fold up chairs lined up against one wall. Babygurl sat on Sean's lap with Baby Jay, Li'l Tony, and Rob to the left and right of him. Twan and his shooters were posted up at the doors and windows just in case shit got gangsta.

He looked around the furniture-less living room as he hit the Newport to see if anybody was uneasy and smirked when he saw nothing. He knew one of these niggas in this bitch was a rat, and a good one. His immediate squad was good, so he canceled them out. He just didn't know about Sean and his people or Twan and his boys.

"I'm pretty sure everybody knows why I shut the traps down and why we are gathered here. It's come to my attention that it's a rat runnin' around here giving up info that only us in this room should know," Kilo said as he finished off his Newport.

Neither Babygurl or her girls were there when Agent Long put them on game in the first place. He saw the way Babygurl looked at Kiesha. He planned on pulling them to the side to see what that look was about, but first he had to see what anybody in this living room had to say.

"What's good? Do anybody wanna say something? Because once I find out, I promise ain't no talkin' ya way out of it."

"So, you tellin' me until one of these hoe-ass niggas tell you that they got some loose-ass lips, that my money gon' stop?" Illy said.

"That's exactly what I'm sayin'," Kilo shot back.

"Well, somebody betta speak up, 'cause I don't like my money comin up short for some bullshit!" Felony spoke up.

Cassy heard in his voice that he was getting pissed off, so she went by his side to try and calm him down.

Kilo kept his eye on Babygurl and noticed she was focused on Li'l Tony or Baby Jay. Now he had known Babygurl all of his life and knew that she knew something. Before he could ask her what was up, somebody's phone beeped, which he would've never heard if the room wasn't dead quiet. Nobody budged to answer it, which pissed him off even more. As soon as he was about to say something again, his phone rang. He looked at the screen and saw that it was a text from Valerie. He opened it up, and for the first time all day, he had some type of good news. He texted her back, then put the phone back in his pocket.

"Babygurl, Kiesha, let me holla at y'all in the back real quick." He got up and walked to the back with them both behind him. Once all three of them were inside of his old room, he closed and locked the door.

"What's up, Kilo?" asked Babygurl.

"Y'all tell me. Y'all sneak glancing at each other like y'all know something, and Babygurl won't take her eyes away from Li'l Tony or Baby Jay. If one of y'all know something, y'all betta tell me, because whoeva it is, is about to take everybody down." He looked them both in the eyes, making sure they understood where he was coming from.

"A few weeks before you came home, that nigga Li'l Tony started moving funny," Babygurl said.

"Li'l Tony, Sean's li'l brother?" he asked, making sure he heard her right.

"We not sure that he snitching, but bro be missing in action sometimes, and every time I catch him by himself on his phone, that nigga be all jumpy and shit," said Kiesha. "I never paid attention until Babygurl put me on ten."

"The only reason I didn't put too much into it is because it was Sean's li'l brother," said Babygurl, then she put her head down.

Kilo caught it and understood that something wasn't right. She was his ride or die, so he automatically knew something was up.

"Now y'all know if the li'l nigga a rat what gots to happen. I'm not gon' say shit right now, but when Agent Long comes back with his name, I'm putting it on a bullet, and if his peoples trip, they asses gon' be right behind him." He left it at that. Now that he had a name, he could focus on that person so he could get back to the money.

***

"So you really think she giving up the spots like that?" Correy asked.

He, Quick, and Savage were at the main stash spot on Muncey Street taking inventory. They had enough work to last them for a long time. Pablo had made sure of that. He had loaded them down with cocaine, heroin, weed, and guns. Pablo had made it clear that he wanted everybody dead that had something to do with the squad. Somehow, they had gotten the drop on Jessica and had been holding her hostage, using her as leverage.

"Hell yeah. She gots to be giving shit up. The only reason this one ain't been hit is because she don't know about this one. I also think she gave them the drop on Jessica too," Quick said while he piled up the pounds of kush he had just counted.

"Damn, li'l baby grimy like that? Last time I checked she hated bro and that bitch smoked her sister. What happened?"

"I don't even know. Half the time I wasn't even paying attention to li'l mama. I was too busy getting this money."

"Shit, you should've let me bust li'l mama's ass up then. I would've had her li'l ass in line," said Savage.

"Man, shut yo' stupid ass up!" Correy laughed. He fucked with Savage because he reminded him of Quick. He knew Quick was fucked up about Jessica being snatched up because he was constantly plotting ways to get her back. Lately, he had been linking up with Juan and Jose, to do what, he didn't know, but whatever it was, he was gon' ride with his homies.

"So what do you got planned on gettin' yo' li'l mama back anyways?" asked Correy as he busted open a pound of kush so he could roll up.

"I told Pablo that I would make the exchange, me for her, and we'll go from there."

"Nigga, that gotta be the dumbest plan that I ever heard," Savage said while looking at Quick.

"Shit, right now, that's the only logical thing to do, plus y'all gon' be right there along with Pablo's team. I'm just goin' in by myself."

"It's still stupid. But we gon' ride with you til the end."

"So what's the count?" Correy asked, then lit the Sweet.

"We got 150 of everything." Savage responded.

Nobody responded because they heard someone pull up. All three of them reached for their bangas out of paranoia, then crept up front. Correy was the first to look out of the window and noticed the red Camaro sitting out front. Right when Correy was about to let loose on his trigga, Quick got a text on his phone.

"Naw, gangsta, that my li'l dip right there," he told Correy.

He watched Correy lower his strap, but he still looked out the window to see who would step out of the car. Quick was glad that she had texted him because Correy was about to fill her car up with some shit she didn't want to feel. This was the only person outside of the crew besides Pablo, Jessica, and Laura that had ever been to the main stash house. The only reason she was here because after what was about to take place, they were going to need a good lawyer. When Correy finally recognized who it was, he looked at Quick like he was crazy.

"Nigga, what the fuck she doin' over here?" he asked.

"Trust me on this one, homie. With the way shit goin', we gon' need her." Quick walked to the door.

He opened it, then stepped to the side as Valerie walked in looking sexy as hell. All three of them looked at her like they wanted to attack her. She looked around and took in the house, which was barely furnished. She knew what to expect because Quick had hipped her to what type of spot this was. She went to sit at the table that was posted in the corner as she let them get a look at her fly.

"So Quick, you called me over here just for y'all to stare?" she asked as she crossed her legs.

"Naw, li'l mama, I called you this way so we could talk business, but you walkin' up in here lookin' like a million bucks got my homies trippin'."

She knew she looked good, but now that she knew what type of house this was, she was ready to leave and meet up with Kilo. She had already texted Kilo earlier to let him know where she was headed.

"Okay. Let's talk," she said with a smile on her face.

Ray Vinci

Chapter 26

It had been two days since Kilo had the little meeting with everybody to let them know about somebody bring them white folks to their front door. He was nervous as hell because he was pretty sure that Babygurl knew that it was him, or at least had a feeling it was him, that was snitching. He felt like his brother Sean was the only reason he was still breathing, so the first chance he had, he got the fuck out of there as fast as possible. He knew he had fucked up when he let that weak-ass detective finesse him into telling. He tried to think of everything possible to get out of the situation but came up with nothing. The only thing he had come up with was to call Detective Stronbone and lace him up about the situation at hand.

Detective Stronbone had told him to meet him at the Skyline Motel, but that was too close to any one of their spots, so the only place to meet was at the Pik-Nik by the Alison apartments off of Guadalupe Street. He made sure he got there before Detective Stronbone just in case somebody was following him. Sean had been blowing up his phone all morning, which he ignored due to him being embarrassed. He knew once his big brother found out that he was a snitch, it would hurt him.

He spotted Detective Stronbone coming from down the street and for some reason, he felt nervous. He watched as the cop pulled in behind him, then waited for a while. Detective Stronbone already knew the process, so getting inside of the police car was a dead issue. Plus the squad was well-connected, and he didn't want to risk the chance of anybody seeing him talking to the laws. After a while, Detective Stronbone got out of his car then slid in the passenger seat of Li'l Tony's BMW.

When the detective slid in, he put his phone in his pocket and looked at him with disgust on his face.

"Don't be ashamed. You not the only one that has cooperated with the law," Detective Stronbone said with a smile on his face.

"Fuck you, you pig-ass bitch!"

"So what's new with Kilo and his little squad of misfits?"

He hated this white boy with everything he had in him. He thought he was better than everybody when in all reality, he was a criminal just like them. He looked at the detective and thought about telling him to get the fuck up out of his shit, but it was already too late for that. The damage was mostly done, so the only thing he could do was try to save himself.

"They know that somebody is telling, and I'm 100 percent sure that Babygurl and Kiesha knows that its me."

"That ain't telling me nothing."

"I know where they got Pablo's daughter at, and in a couple of days, they should be making a trade for Quick, which you know probably gon' end up in a big-ass shootout."

"So, you telling me that I'ma get both Kilo's and Correy's squads, plus Pablo?" Detective Stronbone said with excitement in his voice.

"You will also be able to get Tree too. With everything that I'm about to place at yo' feet, you gon' have enough power to run this city, so I know once everything is said and done you can get me off of all charges, and I need to get out of this city." He made sure he understood because what he had going on was surely to get him killed.

"I will do everything you asking for, especially if I could get everybody you just named. The only thing left that I need you to do when the time comes is get on the stand."

"Naw, white boy, you ain't say shit about getting on no stand," he said, sounding just as nervous as he looked.

"That's the only way this is going to work. Look, you already in too deep, and I know you want to save yourself, so think about it." Detective Stronbone got out of the car, leaving him to think about what he just said.

Li'l Tony knew that he was in too deep, but he also didn't want to take his brother and cousins down with everybody else. He lit a Newport to ease his mind, then pulled off.

The whole time he was walking to the detective, he never noticed the red Camaro that had followed the detective there and left behind him.

***

Kilo, Illy, Slugga, and Felony sat down the street of Correy and Quick's stash spot with Babygurl, Kiesha, Cassy, Sadie, and Ladie behind them in two vans, ready to ride. Kilo only wanted his squad to hit this lock because he had Sean and the rest of the team watching over Jessica. They had moved her to Sutton Oaks so they could be on familiar ground when Quick came to exchange himself. He already knew that Correy wouldn't let Quick give himself up, so he was prepared for whatever bullshit they had planned.

Valerie had come through with the address to Quick's main stash. He knew that everything that he had was inside of this spot, so he knew that it would hurt them to lose what was in it. Valerie also let him know that there was a group of niggas at all times at the stash spot so he knew it wouldn't be easy. He knew that Correy, Quick, and Savage would be on the southside with Pablo trying to figure out a way to get Jessica back.

Kilo spotted three niggas step out on the porch and felt like that was his cue. All four of them stepped out of the car with their guns at their sides and the girls were right beside them on the same gangsta shit. They crept low until they got close to the house and were spotted by one of the niggas on the porch. Illy was the first to let loose on the three niggas, and even though he didn't hit anybody, he Swiss-cheesed the front of the house with the Uzi he had. The three niggas recovered quickly and were busting back as Kilo and Illy dove behind the line of cars on the street. The bullets were rocking the car that they were behind, putting holes the size of soda cans on the side.

He heard more niggas come out of the house, so he knew he had to recover quick. Cassy, knowing that they had the element of surprise, stood up and let loose on her banga, making them stop shooting and run back inside. Once Kilo saw them run back in the house, he and the squad moved towards the front while Babygurl and her girls made their way to the back. Kilo didn't have to explain anything due to them doing this for a living.

Kilo was the first through the door, not waiting, and he started busting his trap, hitting the first nigga he saw. He filled his chest up with bullets, knocking the nigga off of his feet. Once the other niggas in the house heard the gunshots, they must've tried to run, because they heard shots coming from the back. Kilo, Illy, Slugga, and Felony slowly made their way down the hallway to where they knew everything was stashed.

They were halfway down the hall when a nigga busted out of the restroom. Homie never got the chance to up his pistol because Felony being the last one painted the restroom door with brain matter. The door at the end of the hallway busted open and out of instinct, all four of them dove in the empty rooms.

"How many niggas in this bitch!" Illy yelled to Kilo over the gunshots.

"I don't know, but we got to hurry up!" Kilo shouted back.

It sounded like the Fourth of July inside of the house, so they had to move quick. Agent Long gave them a two-hour window, so it wouldn't be too long before the police came. All of them came out of the empty rooms when the gunshots stopped and let their guns bust on the back room. They never eased up on their triggers until they heard the clicks of their guns. Babygurl, Kiesha, Cassy, Sadie, and Ladie came down the hall, making them feel at ease knowing that everybody was smoked.

"Come on, let's get this shit over so we can get the fuck out of this bitch," said Babygurl.

When they stepped in the room, four bodies littered the floor with bullet holes decorating their bodies. Bricks of cocaine, heroin, and kush lined the walls and duffle bags on top of duffle bags were stacked inside of the closet, full of hundreds.

"Jackpot!" said Slugga.

"Babygurl, Kiesha, go get the vans and pull them as close as you can," said Kilo.

The rest of them were already carrying shit to the door. The whole squad was happy because they had finally got at Correy and Quick's main stash.

After Babygurl and Kiesha pulled the vans as close as possible it took them no time to load up and get out of there. The whole time Kilo was in the house, he never heard his phone blowing up.

***

Correy, Quick, and Savage sat in a plush apartment in the Circle hood on the Southside. Philly and Tidy were there along with Juan and Jose and the goons from both sides. Kush blunts and cups of Hennessy were being passed around as everybody waited on Pablo to show up. Today was supposed to be the day he was gon' make the trade for Jessica. Quick already knew what time it was with Kilo and his squad, so he made sure to keep his mind trained on the gangsta shit that was sure to come.

"What's up, Joe, you good or what?" Correy asked, then handed him a bottle of Hennessy to pour up.

"Yeah, I'm just ready to get these hoe ass niggas out of the way so we can take this bitch over like we supposed to."

"Where this nigga at, yo? We been waitin for 'bout an hour," Philly asked impatiently.

"Nigga, you act like you got something betta to do. Enjoy some relax time, damn," Tidy said, making everybody in the room laugh.

Just as everybody started to relax and have a different conversation beside airing Babygurl out, Pablo came in with big-ass Mexicans with tattoos on their faces and a Mossberg pump at each of their sides. Everybody in the house got quiet, including Juan and Jose, since the two Mexicans had never been seen.

"Mijos, sorry I'm late. These are some people I trust very much, and they are here to help you'll get my daughter back. I knew they want to make an exchange, but there is no exchange being made. They kidnapped my daughter, so all I want is blood," Pablo explained calmly.

"I'm glad we on the same thang, because every last one of them bitch-ass niggas gotta die." Quick then hit the blunt he had been smoking.

"So shoot 'em up bang bang it is. Now y'all speaking my language," Savage said as he set the Drako across his lap.

"Do you know where they got her?" Pablo asked Quick.

"Yeah, that bitch texted from Jessica's phone and said they were in the Sutton Oaks." He laughed because he remembered how Kiesha and Slugga had Sutton Oaks on lock.

Correy laughed himself, knowing that it was gon' be everywhere in that bitch. It was a lose-lose situation, but Correy was far from a bitch and was ready to put his gangsta down just like the rest of them.

The whole room got quiet when they heard Quick's phone ring in his pocket. He pulled it out and looked at his screen and saw Valerie's name come across his screen. He was gon' stuff it back in his pocket, but something told him to answer.

'This is my lawyer. I got to answer this." He put the phone to his ear. "Talk to me."

"Looks like I win again," Kilo said from the other end of the phone.

"What the fuck you mean you won again, nigga? I'ma be there in a li'l bit to smoke yo' pussy ass. And where is Valerie!" Quick yelled.

"You mean my cousin-in-law? She right here. It's a shame what pussy will do to a nigga. Thanks for just handing over ya stash so easy. Now if y'all want this bitch, y'all know where to find her." Kilo hung up.

"FUCK! FUCK! FUCK! FUCK!" Quick yelled as he slammed his phone on the ground, smashing it to pieces. Kilo had gotten him for everything they owned all because he slipped on a bitch.

He said nothing as he rushed out the door. Nobody needed to know what was said. They just followed Quick out of the door, ready for war.

Chapter 27

Everybody was in Sutton Oaks, ready for whatever was about to come their way. Kilo was the only one that was calm out of everybody. He was reeling off the come-up on Correy and Quick's stash, but at the same time, he was fucked up because of the information Agent Long and Valerie had hit him with. He still hadn't told Sean that his brother was snitching, so he didn't know what his reaction would be. Personally, he didn't give a fuck about how he felt. He was about to make an example out of Li'l Tony regardless. Babygurl sat next to Sean, who was mugged up with his two 9mm on the table, ready for war.

He made sure Lexi, Bianca, and Valerie were safe just in case the outcome didn't go their way. He was waiting on Tree to show up before he let everybody know what was going on. As if he manifested his appearance, Tree pulled up one deep in his all-red Lexus. He stepped out looking like he was ready to ride also. Without knocking, he walked right in and stood next to Kilo. Kilo looked at Slugga, gave him a head nod, then watched as Slugga stood next to Li'l Tony. Nobody paid attention to what was going on or was even worried about what Kilo had going on.

"Right now, I'm pretty sure Correy and his li'l team on their way with Pablo and his killas to get that li'l bitch that's tied up in the back. The only thing is, whoever comes ain't leaving up out this bitch, but we all know that. Now what I do want to address is the rat that's tryna bring my squad down," Kilo said with just a little bit of anger in his voice.

He let his eyes land on Li'l Tony as everybody followed them. Sean was the first one to get what Kilo was trying to say and spoke up even before Li'l Tony could speak for himself.

"Kilo, my nigga, you tryna say my li'l bro a snitch?" Sean asked with venom in his voice.

"That's exactly what I'm saying. But you don't have to believe me. Just ask him for yourself. He'll tell you…won't you, Li'l Tony?" Kilo said, making sure he matched his aggressiveness with his own.

"What he talkin' 'bout, Li'l Tony?" Baby Jay was the one to ask because Sean was too busy staring down Kilo.

"I don't know what the fuck this nigga talkin' 'bout! I ain't no fuckin snitch!" Li'l Tony said, raising his voice.

"So, you saying my people lying? You met up with that weak-ass detective on the west side yesterday. If you would've been paying attention to yo' surroundings, you would've noticed the red Camaro following the detective, plus you had to know Agent Long was gon' come back with yo' name…Anthony Harper."

When Sean heard Kilo call his little brother by his real name, his head snapped towards Li'l Tony. As he looked at his little brother, all he felt was betrayal and hurt.

"Tell me it ain't so, shawty," was all he could say.

"The question is, what is you gon' do? Because you being the street nigga that you is, you know I can't let him take the stand on any one of my niggas. Shit, I hope you know you going down too."

Sean never got the chance to answer the question because Li'l Tony had tried to say something but was cut short due to Babygurl filling his chest up with bullets.

"Bitch-ass nigga!" Babygurl said as she emptied her whole clip, then looked at Sean. "Don't no rat got no place in this squad."

As soon as she finished her sentence, the front of the apartment got riddled with bullets, causing everybody to drop to the floor. Glass and bullets were flying everywhere as they all crawled, trying to get behind something for cover. Babygurl crawled to the hallway where Kiesha was and immediately started looking for Cassy, Sadie, and Ladie, who were tucked inside the kitchen with their straps in their hands. Kilo and Illy were ducked behind the couch waiting for the shots to stop. Tree, Slugga, and Felony were already making their way out of the back door along with the other goons that was there. It hit him instantly that there was no way that anybody could have gotten all the way behind the apartments without them hearing. He made eye contact with Sean before he started making his way out of the door and knew he was gon' have a problem with him, but his mind was on Correy, so he slid that to the back of his mind.

Babygurl and her girls was already making their way down to the other end of the apartment block with Twan and his four goons right on their heels. He waited for Illy to come out because he was the last one to get back up with the squad. Once he was linked up with his brothers, they made their way around the corner along with Tree, Sean, Baby Jay, and Rob. As soon as Kilo hit the corner, he let his heata start clapping and dropped a body ASAP. His homies were right beside him, sending hot shit towards the ops, dropping niggas left and right. Kilo looked at Tree, who was scanning the crowd, knowing he was looking for Pablo, which made him start looking for Correy and Quick. It seemed like this bitch was flooded with Mexicans and niggas, but his squad was knocking heads off. Somehow, Babygurl, Kiesha, Cassy, Sadie, and Ladie had linked back up with them, which put Kilo at ease. They stepped over body after body, not paying attention to whose team they were on.

Kilo heard gunshots coming from up top from Lou's corner store and hoped that his goons were laying shit down. Kilo was in a zone when he saw Felony's body come off his feet and stood there as he got riddled with bullets. He heard Cassy scream over the gunshots as she aired out the nigga who was responsible for gunning down her nigga. Kilo was so shocked that he never saw the nigga that came from on the other side of the building that they had just passed. All he felt was blood and brain matter spray the side of his neck due to Illy putting a hole through homie's head who thought he had the up on his big brother.

Kilo looked at Illy, who was smiling like he was loving this gangsta shit. He was gon' say something to him until he saw Juan and Jose creeping up on Twan. He saw Tree rush that way, and he was right behind him. Tree knew that Pablo was right behind his nephews and he was right as he spotted Pablo with two big-ass Mexicans with shotguns flanking him. Tree went their way just as Kilo started busting at Juan and Jose, knocking a chunk of meat out of Juan's leg, making him drop instantly. He looked back and saw that Babygurl and Illy were on his trail as they were both sending muthafuckas home. Tree started busting at Pablo but missed as one of the big Mexicans knocked him to the ground. Tree never eased off the trigga as he gunned down the other Mexican. It seemed like luck was on Pablo's side because Tree ran out of bullets as he made his way up on him. If it wasn't for Sadie and Ladie sending shots from a distance, their daddy would've been dead. Pablo and the Mexicans scrambled behind the apartment block just as Correy and Quick made themselves known along with Savage, Philly, and Tidy.

Once everybody saw them niggas, all of their attention was focused on them. Kiesha and Cassy had met back up with the squad, but Kiesha's attention was zeroed in on Quick as well as Babygurl. Correy and Quick and Savage all went their separate ways, but Tidy never got the chance to split up from Philly because Slugga was already on him, stuffing his stomach with bullets.

"Pussy-ass nigga!" he said she he stood over him and put two more in his head. He instantly looked over to air Philly out, but he was gone. He saw Quick run in a hallway with Babygurl and Kiesha right behind him. Kilo, Illy, Sean, Baby Jay, and Rob were on Correy and his four goons that were behind a line of cars. Sadie and Ladie joined in as the squad tried their best to shred any and everything in the way of getting to Correy.

Over the gunshots, Kilo heard the familiar sound of the police and instantly started looking for Babygurl and Kiesha. He looked around and spotted them both busting at Quick. One of them hit him in the back, making him fold up. He watched as they both stood over him and emptied their clips in him, making his body jump with every shot. They must've heard the police sirens, because they started making their way back to them. The sirens were too close, so Kilo knew the police had already entered the apartments, so his mind was on getting away. As Babygurl and Kiesha crossed the street to get to the squad, a police car was making its way down the block. Babygurl had just made it to the other side, but Kiesha was cut off. The whole squad let loose on the police car but had to stop so they wouldn't hit Kiesha.

Correy and the four goons took that as their cue and smashed off in the opposite direction. Kilo grabbed Babygurl, snapping her attention away from Kiesha who had been tackled by a police officer. Sutton Oaks was immediately swarmed with cops so the squad had to get up out of their one way or the other. Kilo, Babygurl, Illy, and Slugga made their way back to the apartment so they could make their exit. Babygurl looked back to see why Cassy, Sadie, and Ladie weren't behind them and saw Tree and Twan pull up on them as Sadie and Ladie jumped in the side of the van they were in. Tree was waiting on Cassy to get in, but her focus was on Kiesha, who was being put in the back of the squad car. She raised her strap to bust at the law that had Kiesha but was stopped by Detective Stronbone with his gun to her head.

Tree peeled off as the rest of the squad watched Cassy lay it down. It hurt Babygurl to leave her girls hanging, but they had to burn out before they were in the same predicament.

There was no sign of Sean and his people, but that was the least of their worries as they ran to the back where their rides was. From down the street, they saw police cars surrounding the apartment so their cars was out of the question.

Kilo wasted no time and made his way toward the train tracks with his squad right behind him.

Ray Vinci

Chapter 28
Six months later

She made her way down Fredricksberg to complete her last mission for Kilo. It was the last thing on his mind when she had brought it up to him. He immediately shut her plan down, but she was determined to finish what she had started so he had finally agreed.

Valerie had been meeting up with Detective Stronbone for the last few months and today was the day that the plan was to come together. Detective Stronbone was the lead detective on Kiesha's and Cassy's case, so he had to be dealt with. They also had to find Jessica, who was a lead witness, but didn't worry too much about her because Kilo knew that Pablo wouldn't let her get on the stand. The police had found her in an apartment butt naked and tied up in the back room and she was safely returned to her mom and dad.

She turned into Budget Suites and parked next to Detective Stronbone's unmarked car. She checked her appearance in the mirror and saw nothing but flawlessness. She texted Kilo, who was parked in the front of the apartment with Babygurl. As soon as she had him where she needed him, they would come in and finish the job. Valerie stepped out of the rental car, then walked up to the door and knocked twice and was immediately let in by the detective.

"I hope you ready for the best time of your life," she said as she walked in, making sure she touched nothing.

"You damn right, sexy mama," he said back excitedly, then sat at the edge of the bed.

"Strip." She dug in her bag and pulled out four black scarfs. "We about to have some fun."

He wasted no time coming out of his clothes and as soon as he was butt naked, he slid back until his back rested on the headboard. She came out of the trench coat she had on and he was rewarded with just her bra and thong. She climbed on top of him as she tied up both his hands, then moved down to tie up his legs.

"You gon' let mama ride this dick to death?" she asked as she jacked him off slowly.

"You can do whatever you like to this dick," he replied, not knowing this would be his last sexual encounter.

She sped up once she saw his face get red and in no time, he was cumming all over her hand and his stomach. He relaxed as she got off the bed.

"Now that you are relaxed a bit, let me wash up." She grabbed her bag then went into the restroom.

He was excited that this young white girl was all over him and he couldn't wait to finally fuck the shit out of her. He was so deep in thought that he didn't hear the door open until Kilo and Babygurl were already on him.

"It's a damn shame how a muthafucka can get caught up trying to get a piece of pussy," Kilo said with his strap to his temple.

Valerie came out of the restroom with the trench coat on and looked at Detective Stronbone, then shook her head.

"This whole time you was setting me up! You dirty bitch! I ought to kill you!" he yelled while he shook, trying to get loose.

"Bitch! Shut up! You ain't even in the position to be making no threats," Babygurl said. "Thanks, Val, we got this."

Valerie walked out of the room as she heard him plead for his life. Nothing else was said. She heard multiple silenced shots. Her mission was complete, and they were one step closer to freeing Kiesha and Cassy.

***

Correy, Philly, and Savage sat in Chacho's off of Perrin Bietle Road along with Pablo, trying to figure out their next move. For the last six months, the streets had been quiet, so it was time for them to get back to the money. Kilo had peeled them for everything they had, but Pablo was there to put them back up to boss status.

They were deep in conversation when Correy thought he spotted a familiar face walking his way. When he noticed the three dread head niggas walk his way, he instantly reached for his heat.

"Nigga, you must don't think we'll splatter y'all ass across Chacho's walls," Correy said, making Philly, Savage, and Pablo look at the three niggas.

"Naw. shawty it ain't even like that. I'm here because we now have beef with the same nigga." Sean explained everything to them, and Correy was loving what he was hearing.

Shit was already working in his favor, so he began to put a plan together to take over the grimy streets of San Antonio. He refused to bow down to Kilo, and wouldn't stop until the streets were his or one of them was dead.

To Be Continued...
Grimey Ways 4
Coming Soon

Ray Vinci

Lock Down Publications and Ca$h Presents assisted
publishing packages.

BASIC PACKAGE $499
Editing
Cover Design
Formatting

UPGRADED PACKAGE $800
Typing
Editing
Cover Design
Formatting

ADVANCE PACKAGE $1,200
Typing
Editing
Cover Design
Formatting
Copyright registration
Proofreading
Upload book to Amazon

LDP SUPREME PACKAGE $1,500
Typing
Editing
Cover Design
Formatting
Copyright registration
Proofreading
Set up Amazon account
Upload book to Amazon
Advertise on LDP Amazon and Facebook page

***Other services available upon request. Additional charges may apply
Lock Down Publications
P.O. Box 944
Stockbridge, GA 30281-9998
Phone # 470 303-9761

Submission Guideline

Submit the first three chapters of your completed manuscript to ldpsubmissions@gmail.com, subject line: Your book's title. The manuscript must be in a .doc file and sent as an attachment. Document should be in Times New Roman, double spaced and in size 12 font. Also, provide your synopsis and full contact information. If sending multiple submissions, they must each be in a separate email.

Have a story but no way to send it electronically? You can still submit to LDP/Ca$h Presents. Send in the first three chapters, written or typed, of your completed manuscript to:

LDP: Submissions Dept
Po Box 944
Stockbridge, Ga 30281

DO NOT send original manuscript. Must be a duplicate.

Provide your synopsis and a cover letter containing your full contact information.

Thanks for considering LDP and Ca$h Presents.

<u>NEW RELEASES</u>

BODYMORE KINGPINS by ROMELL TUKES

LOVE IN THE TRENCHES by COREY ROBINSON

THE COCAINE PRINCESS 7 by KING RIO

GRIMEY WAYS 3 by RAY VINCI

STRAIGHT BEAST MODE III

De'Kari

KINGPIN KILLAZ IV

STREET KINGS III

PAID IN BLOOD III

CARTEL KILLAZ IV

DOPE GODS III

Hood Rich

SINS OF A HUSTLA II

ASAD

YAYO V

Bred In The Game 2

S. Allen

THE STREETS WILL TALK II

By Yolanda Moore

SON OF A DOPE FIEND III

HEAVEN GOT A GHETTO II

SKI MASK MONEY II

By Renta

LOYALTY AIN'T PROMISED III

By Keith Williams

I'M NOTHING WITHOUT HIS LOVE II

SINS OF A THUG II

TO THE THUG I LOVED BEFORE II

IN A HUSTLER I TRUST II

By Monet Dragun

QUIET MONEY IV

EXTENDED CLIP III

THUG LIFE IV

By **Trai'Quan**

THE STREETS MADE ME IV

By **Larry D. Wright**

IF YOU CROSS ME ONCE III

ANGEL V

By **Anthony Fields**

THE STREETS WILL NEVER CLOSE IV

By **K'ajji**

HARD AND RUTHLESS III

KILLA KOUNTY IV

By **Khufu**

MONEY GAME III

By **Smoove Dolla**

JACK BOYS VS DOPE BOYS IV

A GANGSTA'S QUR'AN V

COKE GIRLZ II

COKE BOYS II

LIFE OF A SAVAGE V

CHI'RAQ GANGSTAS V

SOSA GANG II

BRONX SAVAGES II

BODYMORE KINGPINS II

By **Romell Tukes**

MURDA WAS THE CASE III

Elijah R. Freeman

AN UNFORESEEN LOVE IV

BABY, I'M WINTERTIME COLD III

By **Meesha**

QUEEN OF THE ZOO III

By **Black Migo**

CONFESSIONS OF A JACKBOY III

By Nicholas Lock

KING KILLA II

By Vincent "Vitto" Holloway

BETRAYAL OF A THUG III

By Fre$h

THE MURDER QUEENS III

By Michael Gallon

THE BIRTH OF A GANGSTER III

By Delmont Player

TREAL LOVE II

By Le'Monica Jackson

FOR THE LOVE OF BLOOD III

By Jamel Mitchell

RAN OFF ON DA PLUG II

By Paper Boi Rari

HOOD CONSIGLIERE III

By Keese

PRETTY GIRLS DO NASTY THINGS II

By Nicole Goosby

PROTÉGÉ OF A LEGEND III

LOVE IN THE TRENCHES II

By Corey Robinson

IT'S JUST ME AND YOU II

By Ah'Million

BORN IN THE GRAVE III

By Self Made Tay

FOREVER GANGSTA III

By Adrian Dulan

GORILLAZ IN THE TRENCHES II

By SayNoMore
THE COCAINE PRINCESS VIII
By King Rio
CRIME BOSS II
Playa Ray
LOYALTY IS EVERYTHING III
Molotti
HERE TODAY GONE TOMORROW II
By Fly Rock
REAL G'S MOVE IN SILENCE II
By Von Diesel
GRIMEY WAYS IV
By Ray Vinci

<u>Available Now</u>

RESTRAINING ORDER **I & II**
By **CA$H & Coffee**
LOVE KNOWS NO BOUNDARIES **I II & III**
By **Coffee**
RAISED AS A GOON I, II, III & IV
BRED BY THE SLUMS I, II, III
BLAST FOR ME I & II
ROTTEN TO THE CORE I II III
A BRONX TALE I, II, III
DUFFLE BAG CARTEL I II III IV V VI

HEARTLESS GOON I II III IV V

A SAVAGE DOPEBOY I II

DRUG LORDS I II III

CUTTHROAT MAFIA I II

KING OF THE TRENCHES

By **Ghost**

LAY IT DOWN **I & II**

LAST OF A DYING BREED I II

BLOOD STAINS OF A SHOTTA I & II III

By **Jamaica**

LOYAL TO THE GAME I II III

LIFE OF SIN I, II III

By **TJ & Jelissa**

BLOODY COMMAS I & II

SKI MASK CARTEL I II & III

KING OF NEW YORK I II,III IV V

RISE TO POWER I II III

COKE KINGS I II III IV V

BORN HEARTLESS I II III IV

KING OF THE TRAP I II

By **T.J. Edwards**

IF LOVING HIM IS WRONG…I & II

LOVE ME EVEN WHEN IT HURTS I II III

By **Jelissa**

WHEN THE STREETS CLAP BACK I & II III

THE HEART OF A SAVAGE I II III IV

MONEY MAFIA I II

LOYAL TO THE SOIL I II III

By **Jibril Williams**

A DISTINGUISHED THUG STOLE MY HEART I II & III

LOVE SHOULDN'T HURT I II III IV

RENEGADE BOYS I II III IV

PAID IN KARMA I II III

SAVAGE STORMS I II III

AN UNFORESEEN LOVE I II III

BABY, I'M WINTERTIME COLD I II

By **Meesha**

A GANGSTER'S CODE I &, II III

A GANGSTER'S SYN I II III

THE SAVAGE LIFE I II III

CHAINED TO THE STREETS I II III

BLOOD ON THE MONEY I II III

A GANGSTA'S PAIN I II III

By J-Blunt

PUSH IT TO THE LIMIT

By **Bre' Hayes**

BLOOD OF A BOSS **I, II, III, IV, V**

SHADOWS OF THE GAME

TRAP BASTARD

By **Askari**

THE STREETS BLEED MURDER **I, II & III**

THE HEART OF A GANGSTA I II& III

By **Jerry Jackson**

CUM FOR ME I II III IV V VI VII VIII

An **LDP Erotica Collaboration**

BRIDE OF A HUSTLA **I II & II**

THE FETTI GIRLS **I, II& III**

CORRUPTED BY A GANGSTA I, II III, IV

BLINDED BY HIS LOVE

THE PRICE YOU PAY FOR LOVE I, II ,III

DOPE GIRL MAGIC I II III

By **Destiny Skai**

WHEN A GOOD GIRL GOES BAD

By **Adrienne**

THE COST OF LOYALTY I II III

By Kweli

A GANGSTER'S REVENGE **I II III & IV**

THE BOSS MAN'S DAUGHTERS I II III IV V

A SAVAGE LOVE **I & II**

BAE BELONGS TO ME I II

A HUSTLER'S DECEIT I, II, III

WHAT BAD BITCHES DO I, II, III

SOUL OF A MONSTER I II III

KILL ZONE

A DOPE BOY'S QUEEN I II III

TIL DEATH

By **Aryanna**

A KINGPIN'S AMBITON

A KINGPIN'S AMBITION **II**

I MURDER FOR THE DOUGH

By **Ambitious**

TRUE SAVAGE I II III IV V VI VII

DOPE BOY MAGIC I, II, III

MIDNIGHT CARTEL I II III

CITY OF KINGZ I II

NIGHTMARE ON SILENT AVE

THE PLUG OF LIL MEXICO II

CLASSIC CITY

By **Chris Green**

A DOPEBOY'S PRAYER

By **Eddie "Wolf" Lee**

THE KING CARTEL **I, II & III**

By **Frank Gresham**

THESE NIGGAS AIN'T LOYAL **I, II & III**

By **Nikki Tee**

GANGSTA SHYT **I II &III**

By **CATO**

THE ULTIMATE BETRAYAL

By **Phoenix**

BOSS'N UP **I , II & III**

By **Royal Nicole**

I LOVE YOU TO DEATH

By **Destiny J**

I RIDE FOR MY HITTA

I STILL RIDE FOR MY HITTA

By **Misty Holt**

LOVE & CHASIN' PAPER

By **Qay Crockett**

TO DIE IN VAIN

SINS OF A HUSTLA

By **ASAD**

BROOKLYN HUSTLAZ

By **Boogsy Morina**

BROOKLYN ON LOCK I & II

By **Sonovia**

GANGSTA CITY

By **Teddy Duke**

A DRUG KING AND HIS DIAMOND I & II III

A DOPEMAN'S RICHES

HER MAN, MINE'S TOO I, II

CASH MONEY HO'S

THE WIFEY I USED TO BE I II

PRETTY GIRLS DO NASTY THINGS

By Nicole Goosby

TRAPHOUSE KING **I II & III**

KINGPIN KILLAZ I II III

STREET KINGS I II

PAID IN BLOOD **I II**

CARTEL KILLAZ I II III

DOPE GODS I II

By **Hood Rich**

LIPSTICK KILLAH **I, II, III**

CRIME OF PASSION I II & III

FRIEND OR FOE I II III

By **Mimi**

STEADY MOBBN' **I, II, III**

THE STREETS STAINED MY SOUL I II III

By **Marcellus Allen**

WHO SHOT YA **I, II, III**

SON OF A DOPE FIEND I II

HEAVEN GOT A GHETTO

SKI MASK MONEY

Renta

GORILLAZ IN THE BAY **I II III IV**

TEARS OF A GANGSTA I II

3X KRAZY I II

STRAIGHT BEAST MODE I II

DE'KARI

TRIGGADALE I II III

MURDAROBER WAS THE CASE I II

Elijah R. Freeman
GOD BLESS THE TRAPPERS I, II, III
THESE SCANDALOUS STREETS I, II, III
FEAR MY GANGSTA I, II, III IV, V
THESE STREETS DON'T LOVE NOBODY I, II
BURY ME A G I, II, III, IV, V
A GANGSTA'S EMPIRE I, II, III, IV
THE DOPEMAN'S BODYGAURD I II
THE REALEST KILLAZ I II III
THE LAST OF THE OGS I II III
Tranay Adams
THE STREETS ARE CALLING
Duquie Wilson
MARRIED TO A BOSS I II III
By Destiny Skai & Chris Green
KINGZ OF THE GAME I II III IV V VI
CRIME BOSS
Playa Ray
SLAUGHTER GANG I II III
RUTHLESS HEART I II III
By Willie Slaughter
FUK SHYT
By Blakk Diamond
DON'T F#CK WITH MY HEART I II
By Linnea
ADDICTED TO THE DRAMA I II III
IN THE ARM OF HIS BOSS II
By Jamila
YAYO I II III IV
A SHOOTER'S AMBITION I II

BRED IN THE GAME

By S. Allen

TRAP GOD I II III

RICH $AVAGE I II III

MONEY IN THE GRAVE I II III

By Martell Troublesome Bolden

FOREVER GANGSTA I II

GLOCKS ON SATIN SHEETS I II

By Adrian Dulan

TOE TAGZ I II III IV

LEVELS TO THIS SHYT I II

IT'S JUST ME AND YOU

By Ah'Million

KINGPIN DREAMS I II III

RAN OFF ON DA PLUG

By Paper Boi Rari

CONFESSIONS OF A GANGSTA I II III IV

CONFESSIONS OF A JACKBOY I II

By Nicholas Lock

I'M NOTHING WITHOUT HIS LOVE

SINS OF A THUG

TO THE THUG I LOVED BEFORE

A GANGSTA SAVED XMAS

IN A HUSTLER I TRUST

By Monet Dragun

CAUGHT UP IN THE LIFE I II III

THE STREETS NEVER LET GO I II III

By Robert Baptiste

NEW TO THE GAME I II III

MONEY, MURDER & MEMORIES I II III

By **Malik D. Rice**
LIFE OF A SAVAGE I II III IV
A GANGSTA'S QUR'AN I II III IV
MURDA SEASON I II III
GANGLAND CARTEL I II III
CHI'RAQ GANGSTAS I II III IV
KILLERS ON ELM STREET I II III
JACK BOYZ N DA BRONX I II III
A DOPEBOY'S DREAM I II III
JACK BOYS VS DOPE BOYS I II III
COKE GIRLZ
COKE BOYS
SOSA GANG
BRONX SAVAGES
BODYMORE KINGPINS
By **Romell Tukes**
LOYALTY AIN'T PROMISED I II
By **Keith Williams**
QUIET MONEY I II III
THUG LIFE I II III
EXTENDED CLIP I II
A GANGSTA'S PARADISE
By **Trai'Quan**
THE STREETS MADE ME I II III
By **Larry D. Wright**
THE ULTIMATE SACRIFICE I, II, III, IV, V, VI
KHADIFI
IF YOU CROSS ME ONCE I II
ANGEL I II III IV
IN THE BLINK OF AN EYE

By **Anthony Fields**
THE LIFE OF A HOOD STAR
By **Ca$h & Rashia Wilson**
THE STREETS WILL NEVER CLOSE I II III
By **K'ajji**
CREAM I II III
THE STREETS WILL TALK
By **Yolanda Moore**
NIGHTMARES OF A HUSTLA I II III
By **King Dream**
CONCRETE KILLA I II III
VICIOUS LOYALTY I II III
By **Kingpen**
HARD AND RUTHLESS I II
MOB TOWN 251
THE BILLIONAIRE BENTLEYS I II III
REAL G'S MOVE IN SILENCE
By **Von Diesel**
GHOST MOB
Stilloan Robinson
MOB TIES I II III IV V VI
SOUL OF A HUSTLER, HEART OF A KILLER I II
GORILLAZ IN THE TRENCHES
By **SayNoMore**
BODYMORE MURDERLAND I II III
THE BIRTH OF A GANGSTER I II
By **Delmont Player**
FOR THE LOVE OF A BOSS
By **C. D. Blue**
MOBBED UP I II III IV

THE BRICK MAN I II III IV V
THE COCAINE PRINCESS I II III IV V VI VII
By King Rio
KILLA KOUNTY I II III IV
By Khufu
MONEY GAME I II
By Smoove Dolla
A GANGSTA'S KARMA I II III
By FLAME
KING OF THE TRENCHES I II III
by **GHOST & TRANAY ADAMS**
QUEEN OF THE ZOO I II
By **Black Migo**
GRIMEY WAYS I II III
By Ray Vinci
XMAS WITH AN ATL SHOOTER
By Ca$h & Destiny Skai
KING KILLA
By Vincent "Vitto" Holloway
BETRAYAL OF A THUG I II
By Fre$h
THE MURDER QUEENS I II
By Michael Gallon
TREAL LOVE
By Le'Monica Jackson
FOR THE LOVE OF BLOOD I II
By Jamel Mitchell
HOOD CONSIGLIERE I II
By Keese
PROTÉGÉ OF A LEGEND I II

LOVE IN THE TRENCHES

By Corey Robinson

BORN IN THE GRAVE I II

By Self Made Tay

MOAN IN MY MOUTH

By XTASY

TORN BETWEEN A GANGSTER AND A GENTLEMAN

By J-BLUNT & Miss Kim

LOYALTY IS EVERYTHING I II

Molotti

HERE TODAY GONE TOMORROW

By Fly Rock

PILLOW PRINCESS

By S. Hawkins

<u>BOOKS BY LDP'S CEO, CA$H</u>

TRUST IN NO MAN

TRUST IN NO MAN 2

TRUST IN NO MAN 3

BONDED BY BLOOD

SHORTY GOT A THUG

THUGS CRY

THUGS CRY 2

THUGS CRY 3

TRUST NO BITCH

TRUST NO BITCH 2

TRUST NO BITCH 3

TIL MY CASKET DROPS

RESTRAINING ORDER

RESTRAINING ORDER 2

IN LOVE WITH A CONVICT

LIFE OF A HOOD STAR

XMAS WITH AN ATL SHOOTER

Grimey Ways 3

www.ingramcontent.com/pod-product-compliance
Lightning Source LLC
Chambersburg PA
CBHW071206260626
47162CB00003B/1185